The Orion Trilogy

The Broken Kingdom of Orion

The Secrets of Orion

The Blue Bloods of Orion

Published by Flick-It-Books 2023

Copyright © 2023 by Reji Ex

All rights reserved. No part of this publication may be reproduced, stored or transmitted in any form or by any means, electronic, mechanical, photocopying, recording, scanning, or otherwise without written permission from the publisher. It is illegal to copy this book, post it to a website, or distribute it by any other means without permission.

This novel is entirely a work of fiction. The names, characters and incidents portrayed in it are the work of the author's imagination. Any resemblance to actual persons, living or dead, events or localities is entirely coincidental.

Reji Ex asserts the moral right to be identified as the author of this work.

Reji Ex has no responsibility for the persistence or accuracy of URLs for external or third-party Internet Websites referred to in this publication and does not guarantee that any content on such Websites is, or will remain, accurate or appropriate.

Designations used by companies to distinguish their products are often claimed as trademarks. All brand names and product names used in this book and on its cover are trade names, service marks, trademarks and registered trademarks of their respective owners. The publishers and the book are not associated with any product or vendor mentioned in this book. None of the companies referenced within the book have endorsed the book.

Second edition

ISBN: 978-1-959881-13-1 (ebook), 978-1-959881-12-4(Paperback)

Cover art by MiblArt

Interior art by Nicole Nance

Editing by Sage Santiago

REJI EX

THE
BROKEN
KINGDOM
OF ORION

THE ORION TRILOGY

Trigger Warnings

Please be advised that this book contains content that may be triggering for some individuals. If you have any issues with any of below topics, please carefully consider them before reading this book.

Triggers include: graphic depictions of violence, sexual assault, death, and domestic violence.

For my dad, who said his own death is not a reason for me to "slack off" on my writing journey.

1: Earth

Elenora was expecting the same thing that she got every year for her birthday: a card, a homemade cake, and maybe something from the gift shop. She was surprised when her four best (and only) friends knocked on her door and had nothing in their hands. Vine, Jax, Kettle, and Marko stood in her doorway with the biggest grins on their faces.

"Where's my cake?" Elenora jokingly asked. Vine stepped forward and handed Elenora a birthday card. The card read, "Happy Purrr-day" alongside a picture of a cat in a birthday hat. Inside the card were two tickets. Elenora held the tickets in her hands in disbelief as the card fell to the floor.

"Oh, my god. I can't believe this! How did you do this?" Elenora exclaimed.

"Oh, really simple. We told the general that it was for you and he bent over backward," Kettle mocked.

"We figured that you and someone else can go to that city to celebrate your 21st birthday," Marko said.

"And by someone, he totally means himself, because you two are completely a couple," Vine added. Elenora looked at Marko lovingly.

Reji Ex

"We aren't a couple, Vine, you know this," she said.

"Right, and I'm not really green-skinned," Kettle sarcastically replied.

"Easy, Kettle," Jax snickered.

"We know, we know. You can't be an official couple because of stuff," Vine said, placing air quotes around "stuff", "but you two have feelings. It's obvious, and everyone knows it."

Elenora looked down to try to hide her blushing cheeks, before smiling and glancing at Marko. "Marko, will you go on a date with me?"

Marko smiled. "I thought you'd never ask."

Elenora hugged all of her friends before the group split up so she could get ready. She and Marko were very open about their feelings for one another, but they had agreed to stay out of a relationship until they knew what was going on. Marko came from the planet Kuiper, and at any point, he would be sent home.

Elenora, on the other hand, didn't know what planet she came from. She was the only one from that unknown planet though, this much was clear. None of the other kids looked like her when they came to Earth. She was as pale as a porcelain doll with a blue blush on her cheeks. Her striking silver eyes popped out against her blue hair, which waterfalled past her shoulders. She was shining, and so close to looking human that it made the others jealous.

When she was twelve, the kids of Kuiper came to Area 51. They looked different than her. Marko had green, spikey hair, yellow eyes, and fangs like the other Kuiper kids. He was often excluded from the kids of his home planet, as if they all knew a dark secret about him. That's how he and Elenora came to become friends. Two outcast kids alone in the universe.

The Broken Kingdom of Orion

For their first date, Elenora wore a glittery silver top, black jeans, and her combat boots. She looked in the mirror as she brushed her hair. To any unsuspecting person, she looked like a goth teen. She blended in with humans quite well, but laws are laws. She has to stay at Area 51 until she gets word from her home planet, which for her is impossible. She sighed just thinking about it, but she shook the negative thoughts away as quickly as they came. Nothing was going to ruin her birthday date. She grabbed her lucky bracelet and clicked it onto her wrist before leaving her dorm room to meet Marko at the security checkpoint.

She met Marko at the door of the security checkpoint building. She was nervous, but Marko squeezed her hand in reassurance. They silently made their way into the building where they were separated for a briefing by the military personnel. Elenora was sat at a table and a contract was placed in front of her as a soldier sat across from her.

"You are preparing to leave the base for the evening. You are required to sign this contract before leaving. I will go over the contract with you," he said in an almost robotic voice. Elenora nodded. "You are prohibited from informing any Earthborn of the existence of aliens or other planeters. You will return to the base no later than 0100. Any later and you will be considered a threat to the nation. You will be provided with a car and a credit card. Do not max out the credit card. Any questions?"

"How much is on the card?" Elenora asked.

The soldier stared at her for a moment before answering. "The card has no limit, but if you think The General will care, then it's too much." He paused to give Elenora a small smile. "You will also be provided with a fake ID, but if you run into local law enforcement you are required to call The General immediately."

Reji Ex

He slid the contract over to Elenora and she signed the agreement. The soldier pulled out a small box and handed it to Elenora.

"One final thing, The General required that you wear this the entire night," he said.

Elenora opened the box, and inside was a necklace— a beautiful diamond on a gold chain. She smiled at the birthday present and put it on.

Satisfied with the signed agreement, the soldier handed her a credit card and a fake ID before leading her out of the room. Marko waited with the car keys on the other side. He smiled at Elenora and took her to the car.

"Remember, back at 0100," a soldier said as Marko started the car. They drove off to try to make the most of a day off base.

Marko drove through the desert until they came across a little bar in the middle of nowhere.

"Let's stop here to get you your first drink before we make it to the city," he suggested.

"Why wouldn't we just drink in the city?" Elenora questioned.

"Well, it's a human tradition. A rite of passage. Everyone has their first drink at some dive bar before the real 21st party begins," Marko said. Elenora giggled.

Marko and Elenora entered the bar. It was a typical wood panel bar with license plates from every state nailed to one wall and a collage of UFO sitings, pictures, and news clippings on another. A few patrons were playing pool in a dimly lit corner of the bar. A few people were seated at the bartop or tables. Elenora nervously grabbed onto Marko's arm but he appeared to not feel nervous at all, and that reassured Elenora as they sat at the bar.

The Broken Kingdom of Orion

"What can I get ya?" the bartender greeted with a smile. Elenora took the drink menu and read over it a couple of times.

"Umm…strawberry margaritas always look fun on tv," she said.

The bartender squinted at her. "Can I see your ID?"

Elenora handed over the fake ID. The bartender examined her ID and then perked up. "Oh! Today is your birthday!"

The bartender rang a bell that was behind the counter. "We have a birthday here!" she announced to the bar. The bartender looked at Marko for his drink order. After he answered her, she made their drinks. "On the house. For the birthday girl."

"Cheers," Elenora said to Marko before drinking her margarita. Marko sipped his drink and then turned to Elenora.

"I hope you don't mind, but I was looking into things to do for your birthday. I wanted to take you to this one restaurant for dinner and then I thought you would really enjoy a magic show. Vegas has the best magic shows," Marko said. Elenora was almost finished with her drink when she started to feel fuzzy in her head. She gave Marko a concerned look and he laughed. "You're getting a little buzzed. Don't worry. It's what happens when you drink."

"If you say so." Elenora looked around the bar, trying to steady her fuzzy mind, while Marko continued telling her his plans for her birthday celebration. She stopped and noticed a man watching them from across the bar. He had combed-back green hair and yellow eyes. Elenora immediately recognized him as a Kuiporian.

"Do you see that man over there? He looks Kuiporian," she whispered to Marko. Marko looked over then back to Elenora.

"There's no one over there," he said.

Elenora whipped around in time to see the man as he walked out of the front door. "He left."

Reji Ex

Marko finished off his drink and took Elenora by the hand. "Oh well, we should get going too if we're going to make it to everything and get back before curfew," Marko said. He led Elenora to the car and they drove off.

As they drove into Las Vegas, Elenora was overcome by amazement. The lights and sounds were overwhelming. There were people everywhere. There were street performers and music. Tall buildings lit up the sky and the water fountain danced for them. She wondered if this was the only human town like this or if there were other magical places. The TV shows that she watched didn't show any places like this.

They arrived at the restaurant. As the two exited the vehicle, and Marko handed the keys to a valet. The couple entered the restaurant and were seated at a table. They ordered dinner and Elenora ordered another margarita. They ate their dinners and idly talked.

The date was going perfectly. Elenora's beauty completely enchanted Marko. Everything was going perfectly according to Marko's plan— until he noticed the man walking in. His eyes flickered to the door, and he watched as the man was seated in the section across from them. If things were different, he wouldn't think twice about a man coming into a restaurant in Vegas, but everyone from other planets needed to be recorded at Area 51. Marko knew the chances of two Kuiporians being loose on Earth were rare, so this man was most likely the one Elenora had seen at the bar. He was following them.

Marko didn't want to freak out Elenora and ruin her birthday, so he decided to keep it to himself. He smiled at her as she talked about her new favorite binge show, doing his best to keep his eye on the man and act normal enough to not alert Elenora. Of course, keeping

The Broken Kingdom of Orion

Elenora oblivious to the stalker got easier when the waitstaff brought out a small chocolate cake with sparklers lit on the top of it. Her eyes lit up as they sang 'Happy Birthday' to her. The whole place had their attention on her as one of the staff snapped a picture with a polaroid camera. Elenora thanked them. The waitstaff handed her the picture and dispersed.

"Can I see that?" Marko asked.

"It's not set yet. It's still black," Elenora commented. She set the picture down so she could start digging into her cake. Marko quickly snatched the picture and shook it until the image became clear. To his suspicions, the picture did capture the man in the background. Yellow, glowing eyes stared at Elenora, who didn't notice. She was smiling, as happy as could be with the sparklers shining in front of her. Although the background was dim compared to the foreground of the picture, the man was unmistakably Kuiporian. Marko knew if Elenora saw the picture, she would immediately recognize the stalker. He quickly put the picture into his pocket.

"I have to go to the bathroom. Don't go anywhere, okay?" Marko said. He got up and looked at the man. The man, understanding that Marko wanted to talk, nodded and followed him. When the two were in the bathroom, Marko locked the door to assure no humans could overhear them.

"Why are you following us?" he demanded.

"What are you doing with that girl? She's supposed to stay on base," the Kuiporian snapped back. Marko blinked.

"What do you mean?" Marko asked.

"Did you kidnap her?"

Reji Ex

"Did I kidnap someone from a highly protected government facility? That's your question? How would I possibly do that?" Marko taunted. The Kuiporian thought for a second.

"You make a good point. Then how did she escape?"

"Escape? We got a day permit for her birthday," Marko replied.

"You shouldn't have done that. She needs to get back. Now," he demanded.

"Who even are you? I thought you were Kuiporian."

"I am. What does that have to do with anything?"

"You're…you're not here to take me back?" Marko asked.

"You? Why would I be here for you?"

"Hold up. You're from Kuiper but you're not here to pick up the Kuiporian kids. Is there still a war on Kuiper?" Marko asked.

"I…I've been here for the past 20 years. I don't belong on Kuiper anymore," the man stated.

"So, what's your deal with Elenora?" Marko questioned. The man looked at the door, then back to Marko.

"I did a very bad thing. But you need to take that girl back so she can be protected," he warned. Marko was about to question what he meant by that when someone started knocking on the bathroom door. Marko took the opportunity to leave and get Elenora out of there.

"There you are. Is everything okay?" she asked. Marko took her hand and dragged her to the checkout counter, paid for their tab, and left the restaurant in a hurry.

"Marko, you're scaring me. What's going on?" Elenora asked as they got outside.

Marko looked at her and smiled. "Nothing. I just don't want us to be late for the show."

The Broken Kingdom of Orion

"Oh," she giggled. "You scared me there for a second. I thought someone was after us."

"Nope. Just time." He looked behind them and didn't see the man following. His heart raced. He wished he had more answers but his only concern at this time was to keep Elenora safe. They made their way to the theater for the magic show with no more run-ins. Marko couldn't focus on the show, he kept watching Elenora.

Soon, his feelings of fear were replaced with peace and love. Strands of her blue hair fell in Elenora's perfect face, so she would brush them out of her eyes to not miss a moment of the show. Her face would light up whenever a trick was completed. She laughed at the jokes that were told, and her laugh reminded Marko of flowers budding in spring. She looked over at him to make sure he was having fun, and her silver eyes enchanted him. He couldn't help himself; he placed his hand gently on the side of her face and kissed her. She kissed him back at first but then pushed him away, looking confused.

"I'm sorry," he said. They silently watched the rest of the show. When the show ended, they were the last to leave.

"I don't understand. You told me you didn't want to start a relationship because someone was coming back for you," Elenora protested. Marko gave a heavy sigh.

"No one is coming for me." Elenora looked at him.

"You said you didn't want to hurt me."

"I know I said that. And I don't. I love you. I know I love you. I traveled 4 billion miles to find you," he said.

Elenora stopped walking to face him. "You didn't choose that. Your planet was attacked."

Reji Ex

He looked up at the sky, unable to see the stars behind the blaring lights of the city. He looked back at her. She was expecting him to say something, anything, but what could he say? He couldn't tell her about the conversation he had had with the man. Other than that, he should tell her the truth. He loved her and they were both there.

"Look, I don't know how much time I have on Earth, but…I want to be with you. I would rather spend it with you. Maybe…maybe we can convince them to let you come with me," he said.

"Them who?" she asked.

"Anyone, everyone! I won't leave without you. Or, if I do, I'll find you and come back for you. I just…" He looked down and took her hands in his. "You're all that matters to me right now. If I don't have that much time to be here, then I want to spend that time with you. I'm sorry if you get hurt, but I can't stay just friends anymore. I want to be with you."

They were both here now. There were lightyears between them but they made it to each other somehow. They shouldn't waste this moment. Even if it was just a moment and not a lifetime together, they deserved this happiness as much as any human on Earth did.

"I have an idea," she said. Elenora took his hand and led him down the road. She had seen this done in movies enough to know this was a bad idea but also a massively romantic gesture. She found her way to a chapel that had a 24/7 wedding service.

"We shouldn't do this. This is legally binding," Marko said.

"Only on Earth," she confirmed.

He gave her a half smile. "Are you sure about this? We haven't even dated."

"We were on a date today, weren't we? Besides, the rings that we get will be able to be taken to other planets when the time comes.

The Broken Kingdom of Orion

We'll be married on Earth and will have a fond memory when we get separated," she argued.

"I told you I would come back for you."

"Then this will just remind you of that promise," Elenora said. She smiled at him and he smiled back. They walked into the chapel together. They bought gold rings because Marko was severely allergic to silver. They stood in front of Elvis and promised to "love each other tender" till death do they part. They signed a legally binding certificate stating that they were married in the state of Nevada. When it was all said and done, they got back into the car and drove back to the base.

They made it back to the base before curfew. A couple of guards checked them back in and cleared them. They were escorted back to the dorm building where Marko walked his new wife back to her personal room. Marko kissed her deeply and passionately. Elenora melted into him.

"Good night, my wife," he whispered in her ear.

Elenora smiled and closed the door while Marko headed back to his own room. He pulled the photo of Elenora out of his pocket. At first, he frowned at it because of the mysterious man, but then he realized he only wanted to look at his wife. She was so happy in the picture. It was the perfect moment to capture her birthday. He smiled at the picture of his wife and thought to himself, "Forget about that guy. Just let yourself be happy. What's the worst that could happen?"

Marko entered his dorm room, got a pen, and wrote "wife" on the back of the picture. He pinned the picture to the wall next to his bed and laid down. Marko had a feeling that things were going to be good.

2: Battleship Juniper

Captain Aries paced the halls of the prison on his battleship. His cigar left a large cloud of smoke behind him. He glared into the cells at his newly captured prisoners. Some of them were cowering in fear of him while others stayed stoic, but that was futile. He had already captured them.

"Welcome to the Battleship Juniper. I am sure you've heard of it," he announced as he paced. "I have one mission in my mind. Killing you is not it. It's merely a stepping stone."

"Why did you bring us here? Why did you attack our ship?" someone spat out. Aries rolled his eyes. The stoic ones were always sure their way was right, even if it wasn't. They acted like they had the moral high ground when they didn't. The man that had spoken out was the captain of the ship he had just captured. He had long black hair, pulled back in a ponytail, and sharp fangs. He wore the queen's military uniform with the captain's patch ripped off from when he got captured. Aries looked at him.

"You work for that bitch, don't you?" Aries said. "You're not innocent in your mission and you know it. You chose to attack those

The Broken Kingdom of Orion

innocent planets. You've killed children in her name. That goes against the laws of the universe."

"You're not innocent either. You're a pirate," the prisoner said. Aries took a long drag of his cigar and breathed out a cloud of smoke into the air above them.

"Pirate. I've always enjoyed that term. Pirates take what they want. They rob, don't they?" He stood eye to eye with his prisoner. Nothing was between them except the bars. They studied each other like they were both looking for a weakness in the other. A staring match between prisoner and capturer.

"Yes. As you did," the ex-captain finally spoke.

"What's your name?" Aries asked.

"Why should I tell you? Aren't you just going to kill us?" he asked. Another prisoner shuddered at the mention of their possible deaths. The other prisoner was not from their planet. He had red hair and green, catlike eyes. Aries stared at him for a moment, then looked back at the ex-captain.

"Not all of you," he answered. "Some of you will have the opportunity to join me on my mission. But I must warn you, I only hire the most loyal…pirates. My crew will kill for me, and they have. So, anyone attempting to join my crew in an attempt to assassinate me, well, you wouldn't be the first."

"I will never join a pirate like you," said the stoic prisoner.

Aries leaned back and started to laugh. "You serve a killer queen but a pirate seeking revenge is where you draw the line?"

"Our queen is not—" The prisoner was quickly cut off by Aries slamming his fist into the bars, nearly bending the metal. The stoic prisoner jumped back at the violent outburst, the first sign of fear that he had shown.

Reji Ex

"She nebulized my entire planet!" Aries shouted. "Thousands of innocent lives were taken without a chance to fight! I've only killed people like you. You defend a mass murderer, and I've only killed people that support a mass murderer. If that makes me a pirate then I'll wear the title proudly. It's better than her, who has turned innocent people into a gas cloud in space," Aries snapped. He paused, taking a deep breath to collect himself.

He looked at the prisoners that he had. They all looked at him with fear now. He straightened his jacket.

"My name is Captain Aries. I am on a mission to get revenge on the woman that destroyed my entire life. You can join me if you pledge your loyalty to me, but note, I do not keep prisoners. Die with her or fight with me," he said. He turned on his heels and walked, dropping his cigar and stepping on it on his way out.

Aries made his way to the captain's deck. His crew saluted him as he entered the room. He wasn't quite sure who started that trend, but he didn't mind. They were pirates, not a militia. He sat in his chair and stared out of the front window into the vast void. He wondered where she was. He had been on her trail for years. Was she running from him?

How many planets had she destroyed since they last saw each other? What was her plan other than chaos?

"Captain, where do we set our course?" the navigator asked Aries. Aries thought for a moment. He had no idea where to go next, but he was too far deep into his plan for revenge— he couldn't stop now. The truth was that he didn't want this violent life. He wanted what he had before this, what she stole from him.

"Set course to Canis Major. She's not on this side of the galaxy," Aries ordered. Aries stood up and walked over to the window to

The Broken Kingdom of Orion

watch the ship next to theirs burn. He noticed how close its model was to his own ship. The only notable difference was her symbol painted proudly on the side. He knew they would have lived free if they hadn't advertised the killer's logo. He gave himself the same talk that he did every time he ordered an attack that ended lives, "How many planets of people did you save by taking them out?"

Aries no longer felt the jerk of the overdrive starting the hyperjump that propelled the ship through space. He had never flown in a ship before the attack, and since the attack… he hadn't set foot on a planet. He missed it. He wanted to stop jumping from quadrant to quadrant in the galaxy. The problem is, he would never feel safe until *she* was gone. He had to keep hunting her. Maybe she was hunting him too. Aries left the deck and went to his quarters.

The room was dark. There was only one lamp in the room and it didn't provide much light. He didn't mind it. It set the tone for his new personality. He sat at his desk and read over his charts. He placed an x over the area that they had just hyper-jumped from. The map was covered with x's and no results. He sighed.

He reached into his desk and pulled out his wedding photo. His hair was shorter then, and he was permanently smiling. The dark circles that he had now weren't there yet. He wore a purple suit that matched her deep, flowing gown. He was laughing in the picture and putting flowers in her hair. She was smiling with her eyes closed. That night, they gave themselves to each other. He had fully devoted himself to her and her happiness. His heart and his kingdom were hers to rule how she saw fit, and for some unknown reason, she thought turning it into a gas cloud was the direction she wanted to go.

He hated how bitter he was. This wasn't him. This was what she made him into. He desperately wanted to turn her into what she turned his planet into. He knew it wouldn't fix anything. It wouldn't bring them back. But it was enough for him to know she would never hurt anyone ever again. He clung to the picture and lay down on his cot. He slowly fell asleep and dreamed of the day he first met her.

He was seated next to his father, like any other day, when she was brought in. She was escorted in with her family behind her. She wore a strapless gold and red dress with a long, red veil that dragged on the floor behind her. Her beauty instantly caused Aries to perk up and give her his full attention. She floated across the room and kneeled before Aries's father, but she glanced at Aries and smiled. Her parents stood at the front of the room, but Aries hardly noticed them.

"Introducing Princess Nava Nui of Helix," the royal announcer said. The king stood and raised his arms outward in greeting.

"This is a joyous occasion! I welcome our new visitors with open arms, as should you," he announced to the crowd that came to see the new princess. The crowd cheered for her.

Aries courted her. He was his best self around her. The whole planet treated her like a queen. The whole planet was given to her.

When he woke, Aries wiped away the tears that had fallen during his sleep and started his day. He wore black pants with a white shirt and black boots.

Stereotyped pirates from stories old was the narrative he was going for. The people of space feared him as a pirate anyways. He didn't care. It was fun to pretend.

He walked down to the interrogation rooms. This was the day that he had to sort out which prisoners would stay on his ship and who would leave. He sat down at the table and two of his crew members brought a prisoner in chains to sit across from him. When the prisoner was secured, they sat at either corner of the room behind him.

"Name?" Aries demanded, not even looking up from his notebook.

"B-Besnik," the prisoner muttered. Aries sighed in frustration which caused the prisoner to jump in fear.

"I don't like starting my day with the scared ones. It just ruins my mood for the rest of the day," Aries said. Besnik trembled before him. "What did she even want with you anyways? What is your special skill that she needed so badly that she overlooked the rest of you?"

"I…I snuck on the ship. They didn't know that I was there. I was working in the hospital ward without them noticing," Besnik answered. Aries frowned.

"You snuck on their ship? Why?" he asked. Besnik looked down, his hands trembling in fear.

"They…they blew up my planet. I snuck on so I could live. Then, you blew up their ship," Besnik explained. Aries froze when he realized, maybe Besnik wasn't naturally a coward. He was more likely traumatized. He already showed that he's sneaky, clever, and resourceful by sneaking onto an enemy ship and posing as a hospital worker. Aries looked to his guards and nodded to them.

"No...no… please," Besnik protested as the guards closed in on him. His silver chains were unlocked and dropped to the table.

"I-I don't understand. You don't take prisoners," Besnik said. Aries waved his hand and wrote in his notebook.

"I don't. No one will hear about this. They'll take you to the escape pods and a crew member will take you wherever you want. I

Reji Ex

don't care where, just don't ever tell anyone that you saw me. Got it?" Aries demanded.

"Wait. I owe you something," he said.

"You have nothing to give me," Aries pointed out.

"I can work for you. I'm not much of a fighter, but every war needs medical personnel. Right?" Besnik said. Aries thought for a moment and shrugged.

"I only have one med person on board. Maybe you're right. Take him to meet Doc," Aries said to his guards. They led Besnik out of the room without another word and the next prisoner was brought in. The ex-captain was next and his chains were locked to the table.

"Let me guess. You're choosing death?" Aries mocked.

"I didn't say that," the prisoner muttered.

"I cannot take crew members that are loyal to the dark queen," Aries said.

"What do I get in return?"

"Oh, your loyalty is bought?" Aries looked at him, but the man's gaze remained fixed on his hands chained to the table.

"There's a camp for children whose planets are at war. Queen Nava has been attacking peaceful planets. I can't deny that. I worry she'll go after the children. Can we work together to protect the children?" he asked.

"What's your name?" Aries asked. The man sighed and looked around as if he were debating his next words.

"Roman. My name is Roman. I joined her army because…well…I actually don't have to tell you why. All you need to know is that I was important enough to be in charge of blowing up the planet Helix. But I want to make sure the children are safe," he explained to Aries.

The Broken Kingdom of Orion

"Where are the children?" Aries asked.

"A planet called Earth," Roman said.

"I know about Earth. They keep sending those cryptic messages at random. Don't get me wrong, everyone loves the ice cream recipe but they aren't the best at communicating," Aries said.

"Maybe that's why she chose Earth. The lack of communication with other planets would keep the children hidden," Roman suggested.

Aries nodded to the guards, got up, and left. He made his way to the captain's deck. He typed on a computer to get coordinates to Earth. The planet was not too far from their current location.

"Can we take a small detour to this planet?" he asked his navigator.

"Yes, sir," the navigator said as he began to steer the ship in the right direction.

"We will be going to war soon. According to one of the prisoners, the queen might be aiming to attack a children's safety camp," Aries announced.

"We will be ready when you are, captain," the artillery director said. Aries stood at the front of the ship and watched the stars and planets pass him by. He told himself what he always did, "How many innocent planets have you saved by destroying her army?"

He worried Roman's words were a false lead. Perhaps Earth would attack his ship before he could help, or worse. But if innocent children were at risk, then he needed to at least try to help them.

3: Earth

Elenora woke up and started her day like normal. She put on a new shirt, her jeans, and her combat boots, and went down to the cafeteria to meet up with her friends and her husband. She hummed to herself the entire way there. Marko met up with her, laced his fingers with hers, and kissed her cheek.

"Good morning, my princess. How did you sleep?" he asked her.

"I slept great. How are you?"

"I woke up to your picture, so my day started out fantastic," he said.

"Ugh, please don't be one of those couples," Jax groaned as he and the rest of the friend group walked up to them. Jax had cat-like eyes and fiery red hair. He came to Earth alone, kind of like Elenora. Because of that, he had quickly been accepted in their group of outcasts.

"I think it's cute," Vine said. Her snow-white hair was tied up in a high ponytail that bounced with each step she took. Her ears were pointy, and her eyes were very large and entirely dark green.

"A Makemakian would," Kettle replied. The friends grabbed their breakfast, sat at a table, and started eating. Elenora couldn't help but notice the stares and whispers from the other people in the room. She looked down at her food and ate silently.

"They're just jealous," Vine said quietly.

"I know," Elenora whispered back, but she didn't believe that. She knew what everyone said about her. She looked very human compared to the others that were in Area 51. Some people had larger than normal eyes or were extra tall. Some had sharp teeth or cat-like pupils. Some even had grey or blue or green skin that would make them stand out in a crowd of Earth humans. Elenora was simply pale and had blue hair.

"They think the General likes her the best because she's the most human looking, but it's because she has no planet," Kettle commented.

"Kettle," Marko scolded.

Elenora gave Marko a side glance. It was always suggested that she was favored because she was planet-less but that wasn't truly the case. Marko and Vine were the only ones that knew the truth, but Elenora made them promise not to talk about it. Before The General was in charge of Area 51 there had been a different general, General Jonathan Volkov. General Volkov was not fond of the idea of 'aliens' being on Earth. Elenora was the first to visit Earth and stay, so General Volkov took it upon himself to figure out how aliens work, using a similar method to animal testing. Volkov had disappeared mysteriously, then The General took over and took pity on Elenora. He reformed Area 51 to be more accepting and even tried to get rid of the use of the word "alien" to make the Earth people more welcoming to those from other planets.

"Well, it's true. She's Earthian…Earthly…Earthiopian. From Earth," Kettle rambled.

Reji Ex

"Well, we do have some news. We got married yesterday while we were out," Marko announced, desperate to change the subject. Vine squealed with joy.

"That is so cute! But what happens when...oh, nevermind, that's still cute." She looked down at her food and mixed it around, avoiding the uncomfortable topic of Marko leaving. Marko and Elenora didn't mind because they had discussed it.

"So, how was the city?" Jax asked, attempting to change the subject.

"It was brilliant! There were water shows and lights and music." Marko told them all about their trip outside and how beautiful the wedding was. They talked until two army men came up to the table.

"You are being requested by The General," one of them announced, looking at Elenora.

"Me? Why? Am I in trouble?" she asked. They didn't answer her. They gently pulled her up and guided her out of the cafeteria. She looked back at her friends who watched with concern. They all had learned quickly, upon arrival to Area 51, to stay out of the way of the military. The stares from the other people and gossiping whispers increased as Elenora was dragged away. She was desperate to be invisible at that moment, but there was no such luck. She hung her head as she was led away to see The General.

The General's office reminded her of a classic 90's military tv show. There was a big oak desk in the dead center of the room with one of those green lamps sitting on top. Bookshelves lined the walls with unread books living on them. The General sat at his desk and was writing reports when they walked into the room. He looked up at Elenora over his reading glasses. He was your run-of-the-mill, stereotypical, military leader. He had a high fade etched into his salt

The Broken Kingdom of Orion

and pepper hair, a large build, and a no-nonsense scowl permanently imprinted on his face. He pulled a piece of paper out of the desk drawer and handed it to Elenora. The General dismissed the two soldiers that had brought her in.

"Would you care to explain this?" he asked her. His voice boomed without trying, but Elenora was used to him. Elenora looked down at the paper in her hands, then back to The General.

"It's a marriage license," she muttered. The General leaned back in his chair.

"And explain it," he responded calmly. The General stared at her as an intimidation tactic. She was used to this, so she just sat in the swivel chair in front of the desk. The General acted as a father figure to her and that's exactly how she saw him.

"It's only valid on Earth," she said.

"So, when he leaves, what will happen?"

"He says he'll be back for me." Elenora looked at The General and he sighed. He had always had a soft spot for Elenora— ever since he was promoted and put in charge of Area 51. He hated disappointing her.

"Elenora, every child that leaves here leaves with conditions. I can't just allow you to go with him," The General explained. Elenora looked down.

"What planet am I from?"

The General hated this line. Elenora always seemed to ask him this whenever she was in trouble or being told bad news. Was it emotional manipulation? Absolutely, and it worked every time. The General could not disappoint his pseudo-daughter. She was a rare case. She was brought to Earth by herself by someone who didn't come from the same planet as her. The General didn't know where she truly came from. Although the man that had brought her did leave paperwork. The planet written on the form didn't make sense, so it had been kept confidential.

The other children got to leave when their own planets were safe enough. Elenora didn't even know where she came from. No one did. So, she couldn't leave until they had word from the person that had brought her here in the first place. Unfortunately, his identity was secret too. The General didn't tell Elenora the full story of how she got to Earth. He hadn't wanted to upset her. Now, she's old enough to leave the base and get married.

He sighed and rubbed the bridge of his nose. As a military man, feeling helpless and backed against a wall was not a feeling he enjoyed.

"El, you know we don't know where you came from," he said. Elenora looked down. "But I never told you the whole story."

"What story?" Elenora asked.

"You weren't brought with other people. You were brought to us by a man that was clearly not from your planet. We didn't know how he got ahold of you, but he made us promise not to let anyone take you except for one person. We have to honor that promise. So even if Marko did come back for you…we can't let you leave with him. We think your real family is looking for you," he explained.

"My…my real family is looking for me? I thought I was abandoned."

"To avoid stress amongst the children we avoid telling them why they're here. We don't tell them about their planets being at war, although some already know this. We do our best to honor their planet's traditions to keep their cultures alive. But, as you've probably noticed, no one's been leaving Earth. They've all stayed here well into adulthood," The General explained as he stared out his window.

"That's why you have that human program. To teach some of us how to be human without drawing suspicion," Elenora concluded.

"Right. Earth is a bigger planet than some of the other planets that send their people here. We have many different cultures. When they pass our test, they get placed in a culture that best suits their own. Earth is full of people from other planets. No one even knows or bats an eye at them."

"Why are you telling me all this?" Elenora asked. The General looked at her.

"Because there's a high chance that Marko will leave. But you…you're more likely to go live on Earth."

"So we're meant to be separated. That's why you're upset that we got married?"

The General closed his eyes for a moment. He had been married once, but his wife passed away from cancer. He remembered wishing he had married her sooner so they had more time together. He groaned in self-frustration at what he was about to do.

"I shouldn't do this but…" He dug a set of keys out of his desk and placed them in front of Elenora. "Here. A wedding present."

"I don't understand. What is this?" Elenora asked.

"Keys to a house. You and…your husband can both go into the Human Training Program. Live a normal life as best as possible." Elenora's silver eyes lit up with genuine happiness.

"Really? You mean it?"

"The program is only a few weeks long, so if Marko's planet contacts us before the program is up there's nothing we can do about it. But if you two finish the program before that, then you can live on Earth freely,"

Elenora shrieked with joy and grabbed the keys off of the desk.

"Thank you so much," she said, hugging The General before leaving to tell Marko the exciting news.

Elenora was so excited to get back to Marko and tell him the good news. She knocked on the door to Marko's dorm.

"I have exciting news," she said as he answered it.

"Exciting? I thought you were in trouble. Soldiers came and took you away," Marko said as he hugged her protectively.

"That's just how The General gets your attention. Anyways, start packing your stuff. We are moving," Elenora ordered. She gently pulled away from Marko and started digging through his drawers to empty them.

"Moving? Wait, where?" he asked. She jingled the keys in her hand. "I don't understand."

"We are enrolled in the Human Training Program. This, us, our marriage, can be real and permanent on Earth forever," Elenora explained.

"I...I don't know what to say," Marko said.

"Don't say anything! Just pack."

The couple emptied out Marko's room and then went to clear out Elenora's. When they were all packed, they left the dorm building to start their new life in the fake town that was set up on the other side of the base. They found the house number that matched the number on their key and started to move in. The house itself was a simple one-story, one-bedroom house with a fake grass yard inside a white picket fence. The interior was just as simple. It was completely furnished right down to the vase of artificial flowers on the dining room table. It was definitely not something one would expect to see on a military base. It felt more like a movie set, presenting the illusion of a completely fake slice of life.

"I don't know how you did it but…I mean, you know I have a planet. You know I won't stay on Earth," Marko said.

"You'd stay for me. I know you would," Elenora replied. Marko looked back at her and smiled. He wouldn't tell her this now, but he would leave and keep his promise to come back for her. Earth was not his home and he had dreams of taking Elenora to his planet and starting a life there.

They silently unpacked their items. It wasn't long until they were officially moved into their new house. Marko turned to face Elenora and smiled.

"So, now what?" he asked. She looked away and blushed. "What is it?"

"We could…make this marriage official," Elenora suggested.

Marko was taken aback for a moment. Elenora was a very shy girl. Of course, he wanted to sleep with his wife, what man doesn't want to sleep with their wife? He was just surprised that she would suggest it first. At one point, Elenora had confided in him that her body was covered in scars. He understood that forcing her to expose her insecurities, even to him, was out of the question. But here she was, offering without needing to be asked.

He took a step towards her and ran his thumb over her soft lips before capturing them in a kiss. She kissed him back, and he lifted her to carry her to the bedroom. He gently laid her on the bed and pulled away from her.

"You can tell me to stop at any time," he told her. She nodded and he began to lift her shirt slowly until he pulled it completely off. He

Reji Ex

ran his hands over her body while kissing her in various places. She gasped and arched into his touches. He began to undo her jeans when she grabbed his hands. He looked at her.

"I want you to know that…I'm…umm… I'm not like the other girls you've been with," she struggled to say.

"Other girls?" he questioned. Elenora tapped her fingers together nervously trying to find the right words to say.

"I'm not… experienced," she said quietly.

"Oh," Marko laughed. "You think I am? This is my first time too, El."

"But–" Marko kissed her to silence her.

"We'll figure this out together. Let me love you," he whispered into her. She felt her body relax into him as he began to pleasure her.

4: Battleship Juniper

Roman resigned in a prison cell all by himself. His former crewmates were now traitors to the crown or gone. He sat in silence, wondering what possessed him to spill the truth about the children's camp to the pirate Aries. There was too much at risk for him to be telling random space pirates about it. After all, everyone was told how Aries had started this whole war, but thinking back on why Roman joined the Queen's army in the first place, what he was forced to believe wasn't adding up. He was only looking for one thing: answers. He wanted to find his kid brother. Aries seemed like a stepping stone to the truth. If Aries could deliver them to Earth, then maybe there would be answers. So, temporarily, Roman's loyalty was to Aries. Aries didn't quite trust him, so he was confined to prison.

Aries was only alive out of spite. He wanted to get his revenge on the Queen. If he found out why she was the way she was then fine, but that wasn't his primary goal. He hated being a killer. He used to be happy, kind, and gentle. Now, he beat the answers out of prisoners and killed them if he didn't want them around.

Aries made his way back down to the interrogation room where his crew took Roman. Roman was an interesting case to Aries. He wasn't like the others. He didn't jump at the opportunity to join his crew, nor did he swear his loyalty till death. It made Aries wonder what kind of game he was playing. A man with no loyalty was good for no one, not even himself. Loyalty was important to Aries. It only took one disloyal person to destroy his entire planet.

He sat down at the table across from Roman. He stared for a moment, trying to make Roman nervous. Roman just stared back. As far as willpower went, it was clear Roman and Aries were on equal levels. Roman refused to be submissive to Aries whether he pledged his loyalty or not. He was the captain on his own ship and losing his hard-earned rank was something he wasn't quite willing to do.

"What planet are you from?" Aries asked.

"Decline to answer," Roman said.

"Hmm, I haven't heard of that planet," Aries jokingly said. "Next question?"

"How did you hear about this children's camp?"

"The stowaway told us. He was found on our ship and we were gonna throw him out the window before he told us," Roman recalled. Aries could tell that he was lying. Besnik did not tell him about Earth. Why he was using Besnik as a scapegoat was unknown, but Aries knew that Roman was lying.

"You were going somewhere before that. Where?" Aries asked.

"We were coming back from a mission… blowing up a planet," Roman hesitated to say the dark truth.

"Why did you do it? What did she tell you?" Aries asked.

"I don't know. We followed orders blindly. Then Besnik…he said they got word of our attack and sent the children to Earth. He said other planets have done that since the first one didn't have the chance," he explained. Another lie, Aries noted.

The Broken Kingdom of Orion

"Yeah. I am fully aware of the first planet. She didn't collect the children from it though. All the children..." Aries started but he stopped.

"She told me that she got the children off of Helix first," Roman said.

"Do you know this to be fact? Or is Earth a set up to kill me," Aries said.

"I know for a fact that there are children on Earth. I can't tell you if Helix...I...I think I killed kids." Roman looked at the center of the table between them. Aries leaned back in his chair.

"Do you know why she would even want to eliminate Helix?" Aries asked after letting Roman grieve for a moment.

"I don't. Like I said, we were blindly following orders. She took the kids off of my planet and so I just asked her. 'Did you take the kids off of Helix first?' She told me she did," Roman explained. Aries knew he was telling the truth.

"I think we're done here. You can go back to your cell," Aries commanded. He stood up, but Roman grabbed his arm.

"Wait, I'll do it."

"Do what?" Aries asked.

"I...I pledge my loyalty to you...Captain Aries. I pledge my loyalty no matter the price. I want to help you save the children of the galaxy."

"How can you possibly help me?"

"I was trusted by the queen. We never met in person, or at all, but I could probably still contact her. I can trick her into telling me where to find her. I know I can," Roman said. Aries looked at his crew members who were standing like statues in the corner.

"Keep an eye on him," Aries said. The crew unchained Roman and they followed Aries.

"So, are we, like, friends now?" Roman joked. Aries rolled his eyes. Roman watched Aries buzz around the ship checking on crew members. He watched as crew members bowed to him or saluted him. Some announced "captain on deck" when he entered some rooms. Roman was amazed by the respect that a group of kidnapped pirates showed their captain.

"What did you do to them?" Roman muttered. Aries stopped in his tracks and slowly turned to glare at Roman for asking such a stupid question.

"Everyone is here because they want to be," Aries stated.

"He lets us loot ships," a crew member said. Others laughed at his joke.

"Surely, committing crimes isn't the only reason why you follow him." Roman was perplexed by their loyalty.

"It was enough for you to follow the queen." No one laughed.

He looked around at the people staring at him. He suddenly understood. They were all people that the queen had violently wronged. Roman nodded in understanding and the crewmen went back to their work.

"So, what did the queen do to you, Aries? You've seemed to make this war personal," Roman said. Aries turned back around and stormed off. Roman tried to follow him but was stopped by a crewman,

"We don't bother the Captain."

"Why is he so dramatic about this? I mean, everyone here went through the same thing that he did," Roman said. The crew burst out in laughter. Roman was a leader on his own ship. He was a trusted

The Broken Kingdom of Orion

member of the queen's court. He did not like the feeling of being left in the dark so much that the crew was laughing at him.

"We don't know much, but all we know is no one has been more hurt by the queen than the Captain," someone answered. Roman felt threatened even though no one had made a threat or even looked at him with malice. He felt like he was supposed to do something to make himself less of a target. They all knew he had been a part of the queen's army. He turned around to walk out of the room.

One of the guards spoke up, stopping him, "Come on. I'll show you where you'll be staying."

"I…I have my own room?" he asked, surprised. The other guard rolled his eyes.

"Yes, everyone has their own room. This used to be a cruise liner before it was turned into a battleship. It's still got all its rooms. Crew members get their own place. Anything you loot is yours to keep in your room or to take with you when you leave the crew," he explained.

"People leave? Without being killed?" Roman asked.

"Yeah, when we go past a planet they want to stay on, they get sent out on an escape pod. This may come as a shock to you, but if you want people to believe a narrative then you got to sell a story," the crewman said.

"I don't get it," Roman responded.

"Well, how do rumors start? Someone has to spread them. No one here is a prisoner. Well, you are, but no one else is," the guard said.

"So Aries isn't a ruthless killer that slits throats if you look at him wrong?" The guard smirked and shrugged. They had stopped beside a closed door.

Reji Ex

"I have to lock you in until Captain is ready to trust you. No hard feelings. Just knock when you want out."

Roman entered his room and was in awe at the luxury that was in it. The bed sheets were silk. The floor was carpeted. There was a golden mini chandelier hanging from the ceiling. His time as a leader on his own ship wasn't half as luxurious as this. He began to envy a band of pirates living on a cruise ship until he realized he was one of them now. He jumped onto the bed like a little kid, burying his face into the mountain of featherdown pillows. He breathed in the lavender-infused scent, finding himself completely relaxed. He hadn't slept on anything comfortable in years, not since he had joined the queen's army. He drifted to sleep without even realizing it.

Aries made his way to the infirmary to check on Besnik. He had to check on all the new recruits to see if they were fitting in well.

"How's our new recruit working for you, Doc," Aries asked, pushing through the infirmary doors.

"He's got potential, but he's a jumpy kid," Doc answered.

"Do you mind if I take him for a moment?"

Doc chuckled. "You're the captain. Do whatever you want."

"Besnik," Aries called. Besnik jumped at his name but came over to the captain. "I need to speak with you. Come with me."

"Y-yes sir," Besnik said. The captain turned and walked out of the room and Besnik quickly followed. Aries led them to a room that Besnik hadn't been to yet; the kitchen. Besnik was taken aback, but

The Broken Kingdom of Orion

when Aries pointed to a chair he sat down without question. Aries put on an apron and pulled out a frying pan.

"Are you hungry?" he asked.

"N-no, sir. Thank you, though," Besnik replied. He hated how nervous he was. The timid animals are always the ones that got picked out of the herd when being hunted. Besnik was always trying to avoid being picked off.

"I used to cook all the time for my wife… before she blew up my planet. What do you know about that?" Aries questioned. He didn't look at Besnik at all. Besnik swallowed as his nerves grew. He had to remind himself that Aries had spared his life. He wasn't going to hurt him. At least, not now.

"I only know of two planets that have been nebulized. Mine and, I guess, yours," Besnik said quietly.

Aries continued to cook, speaking calmly, "You know, I spoke to Roman, and he claims that you knew about Earth."

"I don't know anything about it. I know Roman said his brother was taken to Earth, but that was the first I heard of it," Besnik said. Aries stopped for a split second but went back to cooking as if nothing happened. "Did I say something wrong?"

"If Roman has a brother on Earth, why wouldn't he just say that?" Aries pondered.

"He's afraid of you. They all were. He's worried you'd hurt his brother, I bet," Besnik said.

"He told you about his brother?" Aries questioned.

"He and I spoke a lot when I was on his ship. We were friends, I would say."

Aries could sense Besnik calming down. He was a nervous, traumatized individual.

Reji Ex

"What do you think of Queen Nava's plan? She blew up Helix and Orion. She's captured Kuiper, Ceres, Eris, and Makemake. Why do you believe she's doing this?" Aries asked. Besnik straightened up. He had never been important enough for someone of high rank to ask him his opinion. He wondered if Aries's intent was to try to calm him down and make him feel needed. He appreciated the effort.

"W-well," he stammered before clearing his throat and trying again but with more self-confidence. "Well, it seems to me like she's captured dwarf planets first. Perhaps she's recruiting armies to go after larger planets next. Start small and build up, right?"

"Hmm, I think you're right. Anyway, let's get to Earth and protect the children before she has the chance to harm them," Aries stated. He plated the food that he had been cooking and placed it in front of Besnik.

"Oh I don't-" he started but was cut off by Aries.

"It's a family tradition to feed people, especially if they're emotionally distraught. My mother would never forgive me if I didn't uphold that much of our traditions," Aries insisted. He turned and left Besnik to eat in peace.

As Besnik stared at the plate of food before him, he couldn't help but feel like he was where he was supposed to be. Like the universe wanted him to be a medic on Aries's ship. He picked up his fork and as he started eating, a bit of information clicked in his mind. Aries had said that Queen Nava was his ex-wife. Besnik only knew of one person that Nava was ever married to, and he was supposed to be dead.

5: Earth

The next morning, Marko woke up with his naked wife in his arms. He took a peaceful moment to observe her while she was still asleep. The sun shone through onto her peaceful face. Her skin was a gleaming porcelain white; her cheeks were a gentle blue. She slowly fluttered her silver eyes open to catch him staring at her. He kissed her forehead.

"Good morning. How did you sleep?" he asked. She stretched and rubbed her eyes.

"I had a dream about a flower field. Nothing else. Just flowers," she replied. He smiled at her and pulled her into a hug. He held her against him for a moment before letting her up. She hadn't moved though. She enjoyed leaning against him and feeling his warmth.

"What about you? What did you dream about?" she asked.

"I didn't need to dream. I already have everything," he said. Elenora snuggled into his chest one last time before getting out of bed.

"Let's get breakfast at the cafe," Elenora said. She got up and started getting dressed. Marko watched as she slowly slipped her clothes on. She noticed him staring at her and that he hadn't moved. "What?"

"Nothing. I was just admiring my wife. You're beautiful, and I'm lucky to have you," he said. She smiled to herself and walked out of the bedroom. Marko quickly got up and got dressed. He followed her and slipped his hand around hers.

They left the house and walked to the cafe. Elenora couldn't help but give a petty smirk to the girls who had bullied her in the past as they watched her and Marko enter the cafe hand in hand. The bullies glared at her and quickly looked away. Elenora and Marko sat at their usual table with their friends.

"So, how's married life? I want to hear all about it!" Vine said.

"Actually, let's just hear the PG parts about it," Kettle commented. Elenora looked at Marko and giggled.

"Well, we moved into one of the houses across the base," Marko started. Vine squealed with delight.

"Are you guys having a house warming?" she asked. Marko shrugged and looked to Elenora to answer.

"Sure! Why don't you guys come tonight," she said.

"This is so exciting! It'll be like we're living a completely normal life. Oooh! I'll bring chocolate fondue over!" Vine cheered.

"Vine, I love your enthusiasm, but you need to dial it all the way back," Kettle jeered. Jax snickered.

"Let her have her moment. Marko and Elenora can't be the only ones that have a happy, normal life. Even if it is fake," he said.

"Oh, no. Actually, Marko and I are in the Human Training Program. We are going to be let out soon," Elenora informed him. Jax stared at her for a moment.

"You're leaving Area 51? To live on Earth?" he asked.

"Yeah, we don't really have an outside game plan yet, but I was thinking about going to college for a degree in something. I've always been good at bomb defusing, but I doubt that's needed too much in daily life," Elenora thought outloud.

"Well, traditionally women stay home and keep house, so I don't think college should be on your list of things to learn about," Jax teased.

"I always enjoyed IT, personally. I do the military IT workshops when they come around, but they can only teach you so much," Vine said.

"Well, Vine, you're never leaving Area 51," Jax tossed back with a slight laugh. Vine shrugged.

"I've thought about putting my request in, actually. I don't really feel all that Makemakian anymore," she said thoughtfully while staring into her mocha.

"That's ridiculous. You belong on Makemake. Just like Kettle belongs on Eris and Marko belongs on Kuiper," Jax said.

"Hardly. We belong where we are needed," Vine said. She smiled at the group. "I have some things that I need to get ready before coming over. I'll see you tonight."

Vine gathered her bag and left the group. Slowly, the others bid each other goodbye and went their separate ways as well. Elenora and Marko went to the little grocery store to get food to make dinner for their friends that evening, then went home. They cooked together until six o'clock rolled around and there was a knock on the door. Elenora went and answered it.

"Surprise!" Vine shouted.

"What? It's not a surprise when they invited us," Jax said. Elenora smiled and ushered her friends inside.

Reji Ex

"So, this is what normal is supposed to look like." Kettle looked around the room curiously.

"Normal is subjective. But hey, dinner's ready. Let's eat!" Marko said. Everyone sat at the dining room table as Marko served them their dinner. They chatted for a while before Elenora realized Kettle hadn't said a word.

"Is everything okay, Kettle?" she asked.

"Huh? Oh, everything's fine," Kettle said. He looked down and picked at his food but didn't eat.

"If it's the food, I can make something else," Marko offered.

"No, the food is delicious. It's just…I got my letter today." The room went silent.

"That's…that's great, Kettle," Elenora said.

"You don't sound too happy about it," he pointed out.

"Well, of course, we're happy about it. That means you're going home."

"I didn't want to say anything earlier because I didn't want to bring the mood down, but I leave in the morning." The friends sat silently, unsure of what to say. Elenora was the first to speak up again.

"What's Eris like?" Kettle looked at her and smiled fondly while remembering his home planet.

"I grew up on a small farm outside of town. It didn't have modern tech like Earth does but no one was in a rush. The people were friendly, mostly. Eris didn't have money like Earth does. We lived on the trade system," he started.

"Sounds sweet. Simple," Vine said.

"It was. The whole planet valued the lives of children the most. Even if you hated kids, you weren't allowed to be mean to them or harm them in any way. Children were gonna grow up to take over the planet some day."

"Your planet sounds gentle and peaceful. It's a shame it got caught up in the war," Vine said.

"Yeah, I still don't understand why that happened at all," Kettle said, looking at his untouched plate sadly.

"But hey, you're going home tomorrow, so that means the planet is safe now, right?" Elenora implored.

"Yeah, but I am gonna miss you guys." The friends had a nice evening reminiscing on their own home planets until it began to get late. They finished their dinners and got ready to leave. Elenora got up and hugged Kettle.

"I won't forget you," she said. He hugged her back.

"I know you won't. I'm sorry, El. I know how hard it is to make friends here. I know it's harder to make friends knowing they'll just leave. But, thank you."

"For what?"

"For being a good friend to me. I really don't know what I would do without you. You're a good girl. Marko is lucky to have you as a wife," Kettle said. Vine started crying and hugged Kettle too. Marko and Jax felt obligated to join the group hug. They stayed that way for a moment before they had to pull apart.

"I wish I could have seen Vegas with you," Kettle added before turning and leaving. Marko closed the door behind their friends and turned to see his wife who was starting to tear up.

"Oh, El," he soothed. He held her while she cried. Neither one said anything for the rest of the night. Marko held his wife until she fell asleep in his arms. He really didn't know how she would react

Reji Ex

when he got his letter. He still didn't have the heart to tell her he wouldn't stay.

The next morning, Elenora and Marko went to see Kettle off for the last time.

"So, this is it. This is the last time I'll see you guys," Kettle said.

"Kettle! You're gonna make me cry again," Vine wailed.

"Well, I'm being honest," Kettle jabbed back.

"I don't really think that's entirely true, Kettle," Elenora said. "I mean, you know Vine is on Makemake, and Marko and I will be on Earth. We're reachable. I know you said Eris was a little behind on technology, but that doesn't mean that it's impossible for one of us to find you."

"You make a good point. Always optimistic."

"I don't know how well reaching out to other planets will go, though," Jax added.

"Well, it's a good thing we don't need your permission," Vine replied with a laugh.

"What are we gonna do without you?" Elenora asked.

"You will spend the rest of your time with your husband while you can. If my planet is war free, then that means his is possibly next, and so is Vine's," Kettle stated.

"The adults were at war while their kids were millions of miles away becoming best friends," Marko pondered.

The group all hugged Kettle one at a time and walked with him to the meeting ground at the edge of the base. Army men were quick to stop them from passing the barrier as Kettle walked through.

"Erisians only," one soldier ordered. Kettle passed through the barrier and looked back at his friends behind the barricade. He waved at them and started to walk toward the building where he would be ushered onto a ship to go back to the people of his planet. The same people that left him here all those years ago. He felt a mix of joy and sorrow. When he got to Earth, he wanted nothing more than to go home. Now, he felt like his feet were made of lead as he dragged his way into the building.

He looked back at his friends one last time. Elenora waved at him and he smiled and waved back.

He found the strength to leave them behind. He entered the building and found his Earth stuff all packed for him and ready to go. He noticed how he only had one duffle bag, so he knew a majority of his things must have been left behind. He got in line with the others from his planet and they were led to a launch pad. They loaded into the ship. No one talked, but there was the occasional sound of crying. A flight attendant stood at the front of the ship's cabin and gave a speech, which Kettle tuned out. Suddenly, the ship took off. Just like that, he was off of Earth and miles away from his friends.

"Do you really think that we'll see him again?" Elenora asked slowly. No one answered. Space was big. Planets were big. The hope of finding someone is so small.

"This feels like a funeral," Vine muttered.

"No, not that," Jax chided. The group looked at him for an answer. "Earth people do this all the time. It's like...It's like a friend moving away to another country."

"Yeah, but Earth has Facebook," Elenora quipped.

"We're not even allowed to have a Facebook," Vine said. Jax shifted his stance.

"Well, friendships don't always last forever either, guys. We were lucky to have this time with him, but he's off to something better now."

Reji Ex

Marko led Elenora back to their house. He wanted to be alone with her while he could. He knew Kuiper was close to Eris; his letter would probably be coming any day now. He planned on coming back for Elenora. There was no way he would possibly leave her behind. He wanted to get her home quickly because staying with the rest of the friend group was making her uneasy about the others leaving. He wanted her to stay happy.

6: Eris

After four whole days on a spaceship, they finally landed on Eris. The planet was a lot different than Kettle remembered. The major difference was the obvious damage from war. The buildings were torn apart, and the whole place seemed like a ghost town…ghost planet.

"What happened?" Kettle muttered to himself. An attendant was within earshot of him and answered.

"War. This is what a planet looks like when it's torn apart by war. But don't worry. The Queen sent her army to protect us," she said with a big smile. "Eris doesn't have a queen," Kettle argued. The attendant giggled.

"It does now, silly. The planet is under the gracious rule of Queen Nava. She liberated us from the evil ruler that led us to war in the first place," her smile got bigger with every word, pushing Kettle to uneasiness. He turned on his heels and tried to get away from that attendant. He looked for someone who would possibly have answers, but he couldn't find anyone who hadn't been on Earth with him. There were only a handful of the kids that were dropped off, and now

Reji Ex

they were all adults. He tried to look for someone that was here during the war to give him answers, but he found no one.

"Hey! Where are you going?" someone shouted at him. He flinched and turned around. Another attendant with a big fake smile was looking at him.

"I was just-" he started, but she cut him off.

"The film is about to start," she said. She led Kettle back to the group. Kayo found him and clung to his arm. Kayo was his childhood friend, but once they went to Earth she had a whole personality shift. She had been mean to him and downright cruel to Elenora. It was like she didn't approve of their friendship and needed him to know it.

"I know I was mean to you on Earth but…I'm scared, Kettle. Something doesn't feel right," she whispered to him.

"I know. Stay close to me," he whispered back. A holographic screen lit the air. Images of the war began to show while a voice spoke over. The video captured was of citizens running for their lives while an army stormed the streets. The former kids of Eris watched on in horror.

"Welcome to Eris!" the computer voice said. "A planet torn apart by greed and envy. A planet torn apart by war, brought back together by the grace and mercy of our Queen. Queen Nava has liberated this land and now we will repay her by living our lives the way she intended for us. We will work for her and she will grant us mercy and kindness. The same way as when she freed us from war. Long live Queen Nava!"

"Long live Queen Nava!" the attendants shouted.

"It's a cult," Kettle whispered to Kayo. Kayo's grip on his arm tightened.

The Broken Kingdom of Orion

"Fear not, children!" the lead attendant shouted. "Some of your families survived the war! Go meet them and they will tell you how wonderful Eris is now!"

Kettle, Kayo, and the others slowly and cautiously walked through the ruins of their town.

"D-don't leave me, please. I'm scared," Kayo whimpered.

"I won't leave you," Kettle promised. "Where would your parents be?"

"I lived down that street." Kayo pointed down the road to an alley two blocks away from their current location. Kettle led the way to the ruined house that Kayo directed him to.

"Mom? Dad? I'm home," Kayo shouted into the half-torn house. She trembled and tears pricked her eyes. "I-I don't think they're here."

"It's okay. Where else would they go?" Kettle asked. Kayo began to cry loudly.

"They're dead! I know they are," she yelled hysterically.

"No, no. They're not. They just hid somewhere, Kayo. Where would they hide?" he asked. Kayo's eyes fluttered and she brushed the tears off of her face with her sleeve. She looked around the broken room. The roof was collapsed in, and the table and chairs were tossed carelessly to the other side of the room. The whole place was coated in a thick layer of rubble and dust. She looked to the doorway and gasped.

"Their shoes aren't here," she commented.

"What?" Kettle asked. Kayo pointed to the doorway where a mat lay empty. "See? That's where we would leave our shoes when we came in. There aren't any shoes there. So they at least didn't die here. They must have left." she said.

Reji Ex

"Do you know where they would go?" Kettled asked. She shook her head.

"Somewhere safe, I hope," she muttered. "Kettle, somethings wrong. I'm scared."

"I know. But there's nothing we can do now. I think...I think we should keep looking for our families. They said that for a reason, right?" Kettle said. Kayo nodded and they wandered down the street together. Soon, they noticed the ship that they had arrived on had launched.

Kayo was stunned. "They left us here. We can't survive on our own."

"We're not on our own. Come on. They have to be here," Kettle reassured.

"It's hopeless. We haven't been here for five years. We hardly remember the layout of our hometown. And it's gonna get dark soon." Kayo's voice rose slowly as she spoke; she was starting to panic.

Kettle grasped Kayo, looking her in the eyes. "Kayo, stop. We will find someone, but panicking isn't gonna help."

He looked around at where they were. There was no one. Not even the people that had come with them were in sight. "Let's find a place to stay for the night."

"I don't want to go back to my house." Kayo hugged herself tightly to try to comfort herself but it didn't seem to help.

"Well...my house was outside of town. We can go there, but it'll be a bit of a walk and, I mean, what if we get there and the place is blown to bits we would be left in the woods with no shelter or anything," he explained. Kayo sighed and looked at him with big eyes.

The Broken Kingdom of Orion

"Please?" she asked. Kettle looked at the sky and begrudgingly agreed. He did not want to risk walking into the woods while it got dark, but he didn't want to force Kayo to do anything she didn't want to do. He didn't remember her being this fearful. She was always the tough bully that wouldn't stop at anything. She was always trying to make you cry, and now she's the one crying and needing consoling. He was seeing a whole new side of her and it really highlighted the whole "bullies are projecting something" spiel that they were always being told. He finally saw Kayo as she was: a scared little kid trying to hide her fears behind childish taunts. Now, she had no choice but to show her emotions. She couldn't bully him here, because he was her only chance of survival.

They walked down the road in silence. The amount of damage to the town made it impossible for any survivors to live in it. Their planet was small. It was about the size of a single Earth country. The population had been around 1 million people before the children were sent to Earth. Kettle shuddered at the idea of how many people may have died in the war. There were only about 100 kids that had qualified to go to Earth. Kettle wondered if this was some sick game of planet repopulation. He worried that the neighboring planets were going through the same issue and his friends, who were happy on Earth, would be going through this same thing.

"Look!" Kayo shouted, pulling Kettle out of his thoughts. She pointed to a little stone house that had lights on and smoke coming out of the chimney.

"Is that your house?" she asked. Kettle stared in awe. His childhood home stood before him without a single piece of damage from the war. They walked up the driveway to the house. Kettle hesitantly knocked on the door. The door slowly opened, revealing an older Erisian. Her large eyes narrowed on Kettle and she gasped.

"Kettle," she breathed.

"Hi, mom," Kettle answered. She threw her arms around him and held him tightly. "My son is finally home," she muttered. When she finally let him go she looked to Kayo. She pulled Kayo into a hug as well. Kayo was surprised at first but quickly welcomed the maternal touch. She missed her own mother.

"Come in, come in. Are you hungry? Your father and aunt are here," Kettle's mother said while she issued them into the house. She closed the door and locked it with three separate locks. Kayo and Kettle stiffened.

"What's going on? Why all the locks?" Kettle's mother looked at him and quickly led the two to the kitchen. "What's going on here?" Kettle asked, nerves creeping back in over his mother's behavior.

Kettle's aunt appeared. "Kettle! You're home!" she yelled, grasping him in a hug. His father was quick to follow.

"We missed you, son," he said.

"No one has answered me. What's going on here?" Kettle insisted. The three elder Erisians looked at each other nervously.

"We are just so happy to have you back," his mother said slowly.

"We are happy that the gracious queen has brought you back to us," his father added, his voice monotonous. They looked back and forth with each other. Kettle's aunt took out a small notebook and scribbled something on the first page before handing it to Kettle. The note read "The Queen took all the kids. Listening=get to see kids". Kettle read it and glared at the words until they made sense to him.

"Wait...the children's camp was… was a manipulation tactic?" Kettle whispered. Kettle understood that the letter and the weird way

The Broken Kingdom of Orion

that his family was talking was probably because the place was bugged. The queen was listening to them and making sure they were submissive to her. The mother nodded.

"We just wanted to get you back and now we have you. Everything will be fine if we just listen to the orders and comply," his mother informed them.

"So my family is alive?" Kayo asked.

Kettle's father answered her question. "Chances are great that they're out there. There wouldn't be a point in bringing you back unless they could use you to manipulate them."

"My name is Kayo, by the way," Kayo introduced herself. Kettle's mother smiled gently and patted her on the shoulder.

"We know, sweety. You used to make mud pies in our backyard when you and Kettle were five. I'm Argo, and this is my husband, Kojo, and my sister, Elma. You are welcome to stay with us. It's safe here."

"Does Earth know?" Kettle asked.

"No, I don't suppose they do," Kojo said.

"We have to warn them. They're gonna send all these kids back home and their home is…is this!" The elder Erisians panicked the more Kettle's voice rose. Elma looked out the window and quickly drew the blinds. Argo held her son's shoulders.

"Now, Kettle, the queen is kind and we must thank her." Her eyes were full of panic, but she smiled.

"No one's out there," Elma informed them.

"Draw the blinds and let's go to the basement," Kojo said quietly. The family closed all the blinds in the house, shutting out the last bit of light for the day. They walked down the stairs to the basement in a single file. The basement had one dim light hanging overhead but the room looked homey. The family pictures that used to hang on the walls upstairs were now in the basement. Curtains that were for decorations and not to keep light and eyes out were hanging from the corners. There were three mattresses on the ground with pillows and comforters and cuddly blankets. The bed that was obviously meant for Kettle had a childhood teddy bear on it. Kettle placed his bag down next to his bed.

"Why has everything been moved down here?" he asked.

"Safer. The war raged on upstairs and we didn't know if we would be bombed or not. So, we moved everything down here. Your mom wanted it to look nice and not like a basement so the curtains and pictures and vases were brought down too," Kojo answered.

Kettle sat down on his bed and looked at his childhood bear.

"Sorry, Kayo. We didn't know that you would be coming. We can try to make a bed out of extra blankets and pillows for you," Argo offered. Kayo gave a half smile.

"Thank you, I'll help."

Together they pulled extra blankets off the beds and made Kayo a bed in the corner of the room. They sat on their respective beds and relaxed.

"We figured out that we couldn't be heard in the basement. We can talk openly down here.

We don't know if they have listening devices in every house or if their radar is what picks up on our conversations, but we did learn that they can't hear us down here," Elma explained. Kettle rubbed at his neck. He didn't realize how tense he was.

"So, the war isn't actually over. They just have control of the planets," Kettle confirmed.

The Broken Kingdom of Orion

His father spoke up, "It's not so bad. We work for food vouchers now instead of money. We are allowed firewood since we work on a farm and can't have days off like the others to go out and collect it."

"We just can't say what we want, do what we want, or think what we want. Other than that, perfect." Elma's voice was full of sarcasm.

"She used the children as manipulation for a long time, and finally, we were rewarded with you coming home," Argo said. Kettle shook his head.

"So, she's created a dictatorship?" Kettle was still trying to confirm all the changes to his planet.

Elma shrugged. "More or less."

"Well," Kojo asserted, "we should get some sleep. We have work to do in the morning."

"What kind of work?" Kayo implored.

Elma was the one to answer. "We were fortunate enough to be allowed to continue working on the farm. We make the town's bread supply, but I'm pretty sure it's just to keep us busy."

"Sure glad we have two extra hands to help," Kojo said.

"What about my parents?" Kayo reminded them.

"We can send a letter to town when the…" Argo started but trailed off.

"Freaking rabid guard dogs of the queen harass us in the morning?" Elma offered. Argo nodded.

"Yes, when morning check-in happens."

"They don't have an issue with you being locked in the basement?" Kettle asked.

"If they do, they've never said. So, it's safe to assume they don't. Now go to sleep. We aren't the only farm, but we are the only bakery," Argo said.

Reji Ex

Kettle settled into his bed and looked over at Kayo. He felt sorry for her. She was alone on a pile of blankets on a basement floor. On Earth, she had her own room, her own friends, and life. Now, she was trapped, just like him. He at least had his family there with him. Kettle sighed and rolled over in his bed to fall into a dreamless sleep.

7: Earth

Elenora woke up in Marko's arms again. She buried her face in his chest. In the past week, over half of the children had been taken back to their home planets. The General reminded them that this was a good thing, the point of the camp was to keep the children safe until they could go back home, but she was filled with fear that Kuiporians were next. Or Makemakians. Or wherever Jax was from, she could never remember. She was scared her friends would be leaving her. That Marko would leave her.

Marko held onto her protectively in his sleep. She brushed him off and got out of bed, ready to start her day. She didn't have any plans. She made herself a cup of coffee; she wasn't hungry for breakfast. She stared at her cup in disbelief.

She knew the wars were slowly clearing away from planets. Soon, she would be the only one left on Earth. She didn't want to be alone. She had felt alone her whole life.

She looked in the bedroom and saw Marko was still sleeping, so she decided to go for a walk. There weren't many places to go in times of lonely restlessness, but she still left the house to wander the base. She watched the military men and women run through drills

Reji Ex

and training. She walked to her old school building which was run down from lack of use over the last couple of years. She remembered the day that the Kuiper children came to Earth. She had been so excited when she saw their ship land. She was eleven at the time and had no friends. She was certain that this ship was going to have friends on it and there was, Marko. Over the next few years Kettle, Jax, and Vine arrived. They all quickly became friends. It was the five of them, alone in the universe. Soon it would be just Elenora.

A voice broke through Elenora's reminiscing.

"You shouldn't be here."

Elenora whipped around to see Vine walking towards her. Elenora smiled.

"You shouldn't be here either," she snarked back.

"Come on. Let's go somewhere where we won't get in trouble," Vine suggested. Elenora and Vine walked to the cafe and ordered mochas. They sat at a table, sipped their drinks, and talked.

"I knew you would be by the school. You always go there when you're upset. I was looking for you, actually," Vine said.

"You were? What for?"

"Well, I like Jax," Vine confessed.

"Okay."

"And I want to date him, but I'm worried about being sent home after we start dating. You know, like the same reason you didn't want to date Marko. But now you're married, and I just don't know what I should do. Date him or not date him," Vine rambled.

"I understand. Plus, all week people have been getting their letters. It's really risky to start a relationship with someone right now," Elenora added. Vine's shoulders slumped.

"I know. And the thing is, I don't even know if I really like him or if I just feel alone since Kettle left and you and Marko spend all your time together."

"We don't spend all of our time together," Elenora protested.

"Well, sure you do. But it's okay. It's the honeymoon faze," Vine explained. "We don't hang out like we used to and it's fine. I just wish we had more time. Or at least knew when our time was ending."

"I know. I wish there was something we could do," Elenora said. The women sat silently for a moment, unsure of what to say to each other.

"You know, I don't think anyone had actually gone back to their home planet's until this week," Vine said. Elenora thought about that and agreed.

"The General told me that when the kids grow up, they get taught how to be human and let out of the program."

"So, only now planets are being deemed safe to go home to? I wonder if they've all been fighting with each other." Elenora twirled her mocha in its cup.

"I don't know. I wouldn't know. I'm…staying on Earth forever," Elenora said quietly.

"That's not true. You came from somewhere that wasn't Earth. You'll go back there soon, I think." Vine tried to console her.

"I just don't want to be alone again."

"I think… I think the only thing we can do is be happy about today and worry about tomorrow's sadness when tomorrow comes," Vine finally said. Elenora finished her cup of coffee and stood up.

"It was nice talking, but I have to get home. Marko should be awake now." Vine got up and they walked out the door together. They hugged before going their separate ways.

Reji Ex

Elenora walked past the fake houses with their fake picket fences; fake flowerbeds sat in some of the fake yards. She wondered if Earth was really this simple or if this was just some false-hope idea that the government was giving them. She didn't spend too long thinking about it because she had to go home to her husband. She turned away from the fake house and made her way home. She entered the house and saw Marko sitting at the table with his head in his hands.

"Hey. I'm sorry for not being here when you woke up. I was with Vine." He looked up at her. Her eyes met his and she immediately knew what had happened while she was gone. The wind was completely pulled out of her lungs. Time stopped and the world around her faded. Her breathing went from suffocation to rapid, panicked breaths. Her vision blurred and her heartbeat became unbearable.

"I…I was just with Vine," she muttered. Marko got up and hugged her. Her knees gave out beneath her, but he was there to scoop her into his arms. He carried her to the couch and held onto her while she cried.

"This can't be happening," she sobbed.

"I'm sorry," he whispered to her. She wiped her tears away and sniffled.

"You don't have anything to be sorry for," she said. His heart broke seeing his wife in so much emotional pain and being unable to fix it. He hadn't even told her. He didn't need to tell her. She already knew. He didn't want to even say it either. It was as if saying it would make it real and keeping it to himself was just speculation. They both knew. They both knew it was real, and it was happening, but neither one could say it aloud.

Elenora's sniffles subsided, she looked up at Marko. "Let's break out."

"What?" Marko blinked.

"Yeah, let's leave tonight. We'll break out and live our life together," Elenora smiled up at her husband. His shoulders slumped.

"We can't," Marko said.

"Yes, we can! We can find a weak spot along the fence. No one will find us," Elenora argued desperately.

"That's just it. There's one person that would find us and…I…" Marko started. He didn't want to tell her about the man that he had met on her birthday. He wanted his last day with her to be enjoyable, but he knew she'd continue to push the idea of escaping together unless he told her the truth. He took her hand in his and looked her in the eyes.

"Elenora, when we left the base, that man you saw in the bar was following us. I talked to him and he made it clear that you have to stay here. I don't know why but-,"

Elenora cut him off. "Why are you saying this?"

"I don't want you to try to leave the base after I leave," he asserted.

"So, you were letting me believe that we were going to live on Earth when you didn't have the same dream?" she snapped. Marko looked down.

"Yes. I wanted you to be happy," he confessed.

"You're leaving tomorrow and you're telling me now that someone is out to get me?" she snapped. Elenora stood up and started pacing.

"No, no. He's not after you. He just wants you to stay in the base." She turned to him and gave him a look of disgust. "Right, that's not what you want to hear right now. Look, let's spend the day together and have a great last night."

Elenora looked at him for a moment before silently sitting next to him. He threw his arms around her and kissed her cheek.

"We can do anything you want. What do you want to do?" he asked.

"I want to know who that man was."

"Well, you kind of can't. Look, tomorrow after...after that... you can talk to The General. I'm sure he knows who the guy is. I mean, he knows everyone that's come to Earth. But tonight, I want to spend my last night on Earth with my wife," he said. Elenora thought for a moment and then nodded.

"Movie night?" she asked. Marko smiled.

"Yes, let's have a movie night. I'll make popcorn and you pick out the movie. Let's put on our pajamas too, make it a whole cliche thing," Marko suggested.

"But it's noon."

Marko looked out the window to the shining sun. "So what? We can wear PJs all day and then we can stay up all night." Marko went into the kitchen to make popcorn while Elenora picked out some romantic comedy. Marko grimaced as he saw it queued up on the TV, but he forced a smile as he walked into the room with pop and popcorn.

"This looks great!" he lied as Elenora snuggled into his arms. They munched on popcorn and drank their sodas until the sun set. Marko wished that this moment would last forever. For the duration of the movie, they were normal. They weren't aliens that were being separated tomorrow. They were people, normal people. People that other people would call "normal". Marko over-thought that word instead of paying attention to the movie in front of him. Truthfully, anything would have distracted him from the rom-com, but the idea of having a normal human life on Earth weighed heavily on his mind. He kissed the top of Elenora's head while the credits for their fourth or fifth movie played.

"Come with me real quick," he said.

"Where are we going?"

"Just to the yard."

Marko picked up a blanket and led Elenora to the front yard. He placed the blanket on the grass and laid on it, patting the spot next to him in invitation. Elenora complied with his nonverbal request and laid beside him. They looked up at the stars together. Marko pointed at one point in the sky.

"See that? That's my planet. That's where I'll be until I can come back for you." Elenora looked where he was pointing and chortled.

"What star is that, Marko?" she challenged.

"I have no idea," he said.

"Then how can you possibly know that that's your planet?"

Marko laughed with her and they continued looking at the stars.

"I know it's in the sky," he said after a moment of silence. "And that's where I'll be. And I will come back to you. I won't stop until I'm back with you."

They stayed out in the yard, watching the stars until they had fallen asleep. The next morning, they woke up in each other's arms. Army men had walked up to the house to collect Marko's things, startling the couple awake.

"Marko," one of the Army men said.

"Yes, I'm Marko," Marko replied.

"You are to report to the launching pad at 1300."

Reji Ex

Elenora and Marko stood up. Elenora quickly scooped up the blanket and headed into the house.

"Yes, sir. Thank you."

The man nodded and left without another word. Marko made his way into his house where his wife had started making breakfast.

"I had fun yesterday," he said. Elenora stayed silent but put two plates of food on the table. Marko sat down. "This looks good."

Marko took a bite of his breakfast while Elenora ate hers quickly.

"El," he started. She didn't say anything. "You have to talk to me."

"I'm fine," she said.

"Well, the silence isn't convincing."

"What do you want me to say? That I love you? Or that I'll miss you? Because you know all of that."

"I know you love me. I want you to..." his sentence trailed off.

"What?"

"I want you to believe me when I say I'm coming back for you." The desperation in Marko's voice made Elenora's head snap up to look him in the eyes. He was sincere. He truly believed that in the vast void of space, he would find a way back to her. She, herself, didn't have such high hopes, but the belief that he had in her, in their love, in their marriage, made her heart feel a glimmer of hope. She slipped off her lucky bracelet and locked it onto his wrist.

"I believe you," she whispered.

"What's this for?" He lifted his hand in reference to the bracelet.

"It's to give you a little luck to get you back to me," she answered sweetly. He pulled her close and kissed her deeply. She returned the favor. Marko picked her up and carried her to the bedroom where they made love for what they both believed could have been for the last time. They promised their bodies to only each other. Their wedding vow to only love each other for the rest of their days shone brightly in their hearts.

At one in the afternoon, Marko headed to the launch pad with the other Kuiporians. He silently obliged the commands of the Army men until he was seated on the ship. He didn't look out the window while the ship blasted off. Elenora didn't go to see him off. The familiar rumble of a ship taking off shook the house, but Elenora didn't flinch. She finished washing her dishes and then laid down in her bed. She wasn't feeling heartbreak. Her heart was not broken, because she believed in her husband's fidelity and love for her. She believed in his need to get back to her from lightyears away. She believed him, so her heart wasn't broken.

She felt something similar to the death of a loved one. But that wasn't quite right either, because death was a sad thing. She didn't feel sad. She felt something similar to the color white; bright… but empty, filled with so many possibilities, yet blank. The name of the emotion she was feeling had not existed yet, the only word to describe how she felt was…numb. She was no longer a whole person; the part of her that held her emotions had left Earth. She was numb.

Reji Ex

8: Eris

Kettle was woken up by a sharp banging on the front door from upstairs. Kojo was the first to respond, rushing up the basement stairs to answer the door. Argo and Elma quickly helped Kayo and Kettle out of bed and up the stairs.

"Stay quiet," Argo instructed. The five of them stood in what was once the living room of their little stone cabin. Kojo held the door open for one of the attendants that had been on the plane. Kettle was confused by why she was still there if the ship was gone, but he didn't think too long on it.

"Hello! My name is Rose. Isn't it a wonderful day to serve our gracious queen? Today, I am going to give you your food rations. How many people are working today?" Rose asked with a big smile.

"There are five of us here," Kojo said. Rose stared blankly for a moment before speaking again.

"I'm sorry. My instructions must have been unclear. How many people are working today?"

"Five are working today," Kojo replied. Rose's head tipped to the side then quickly straightened up. Her big fake smile didn't waver.

The Broken Kingdom of Orion

"Fantastic! Don't you just love working for our queen? I will be checking up on you throughout the day. Your job is farming. Is that right?"

"That is correct," Kojo confirmed.

"Fantastic! Don't you just love working for our queen?"

"Yes, we do," Kojo confirmed, the script falling from his mouth. Rose turned on her heels and walked away without another word. Kojo turned to face everyone. "Come on, let's get to work."

Kojo led the family to the barn. He taught Kayo and Kettle how to do the chores. There were only two types of animals on the farm, gallus and bostaurus. Kayo and Elma were sent to the bostaurus barn while Kojo and Kettle worked in the gallus barn. Argo was working alone in the bakery.

"Can we talk here?" Kettle asked when they were alone in the gallus barn.

"Would you like to talk about how great it is to serve the queen?" Kojo asked him.

Kettle nodded in understanding and kept his mouth shut. He cleaned pens and gave the gallus their feed. He stared at them briefly and thought they looked an awful lot like Earth chickens. He wondered if chickens came from his planet. Or maybe it was just a coincidence that planets had similarly shaped people and animals. He collected the eggs from the gallus. Elma and Kayo tended to the bostaurus and collected milk. There were at least a hundred animals on this farm. He thought his mother and father must have been exhausted from doing all this work by themselves. Argo was in charge of making bread. She had a machine that harvested the field of wheat for her and grounded it into flour, but the baking was entirely on her. With Kettle's assistance, the gallus were taken care of quickly and the eggs were packed in their collection containers, so, Kojo and Kettle made their way to the bakery to help Argo.

Argo faced the men as they arrived back to the house. "I have to have one-hundred loaves done before the end of the day. If you can start with the cleaning, I'll be done with the baking in time to start dinner for the family."

"Wait, you wouldn't have to cook after working all day. Would you?" Kettle asked.

"Well, who else would do it?" Argo stated simply. Suddenly, Rose appeared in the doorway. She startled Kettle by how quickly and quietly had she appeared.

"Hello! It's me, Rose! I am here to check up on you. Is your work done for the day? It's a wonderful day to work for the queen." The same smile as always was plastered to her face. Argo looked around the room and counted loaves of bread.

"I have 5 more loaves in the oven and then I should be done for the day. "The room quickly filled with other attendants that looked similar to Rose; they collected the loaves of bread from the shelves. As quickly as they had entered, they were gone.

"Congratulations! It's an honor to serve our queen. As a reward, you can keep the five extra loaves. Remember, because your children have returned you will need to make 150 loaves tomorrow."

Kettle spoke up, "150? But she's already overworked." Rose's head turned to look at Kettle, but her smile didn't waver.

"Kettle, that isn't how we serve the queen," Argo reprimanded him, nerves causing her voice to shake. Rose's attention was brought back to Argo.

"Your request for additional help has been taken into consideration. Your five rations have been delivered to your kitchen.

The Broken Kingdom of Orion

Have a wonderful evening, and remember, the queen saved us all from the death of war." Rose turned on her heels and walked out without saying another word. Kettle carefully followed her out the front door of the bakery, quickly stopping when he saw what was outside. There was a truck parked outside of the bostaurus barn. The dozens of attendings that had just been in the bakery were collecting the jars of milk that Elma and Kayo had collected and loading them into the truck. The truck drove off with all of the attendants, all of the eggs, all of the bread, and all of the milk.

"Where is it going?" Kettle asked.

"To deliver the food that we collected to the rest of the town," Kojo answered.

"I don't know what she meant by that. 'Your additional request has been taken into consideration.' Are they going to assign someone to assist in the bakery? You shouldn't have said anything, Kettle," Argo scolded.

"I'm sorry, mom. Things are different on Earth. Very different," Kettle said. Argo took the remaining bread out of the stone fire oven and set it down to cool. "Let's just get these baking pans cleaned and put away, and then I'll make dinner."

The family silently finished their chores for the day and made their way to the house. Kettle sat down in the wooden chair by the table. Kayo sat next to him and put her head down.

"I'm too exhausted to even look for my family after today," she muttered,

"That's okay. You can go out tomorrow, but you'll be on your own to look," Elma replied.

Reji Ex

Argo started chopping vegetables for dinner while Kojo made a fire in the fireplace. The family didn't say much except for offering help to Argo. Argo accepted their help, and soon, dinner was done.

Kojo grabbed the kettle of soup from off the fire, Elma grabbed bowls and spoons, and Argo grabbed the bread. They silently agreed to eat their dinner in the basement so they could speak freely and made their way down. Once in the basement, the family breathed a collective sigh of relief.

"Okay, we can talk now," Kojo announced as he scooped out soup for everyone.

"That was rough," Kettle commented between bites.

"What part? Work or the unwritten script we have to follow?" Elma teased.

"Both," Kettle mumbled. "That girl, Rose, something about her wasn't right."

"They never are. They read off of a script and have to walk in uniform. I assume they're brainwashed or had the personalities beat out of them," Elma said.

"When they come to check on us, you don't speak to them. Not until you understand how to talk to them," Argo scolded.

"Sorry, but you already seem overloaded with work here. I don't see how you can make an extra 50 loaves a day without any help," Kettle ranted.

"I know that but there's a way you have to speak to them," Argo said.

"What happens if we don't follow their rules?"

Kojo and Argo looked at each other for a brief moment. "Bad things happen. They've arrested people. They've beaten people. I saw them kill my friend one day for calling the queen out for the way

The Broken Kingdom of Orion

we were being treated." Argo stirred her soup quietly, thinking back to before the kids were brought home. It had been rough and violent. They were forced to only say positive things about a person they never even saw. They worked for food and often didn't have time to collect other necessities like wood for the fire.

"What about my family?" Kayo asked.

"What about them?" Kettle questioned.

"Well, my mother used to bake. And my dad, I'm sure, could help. I had two older siblings that didn't come to Earth with me, so that's four extra people."

Argo looked to Kayo. "We'll have to talk to the assistant when they come in the morning."

"Wait," Kettle interrupted. "What about food? I mean... you can't do all the cooking and baking. Not with more people.'

"And what about space?" Kojo added. "I don't think the basement could fit four more people."

"Everyone has to make sacrifices at some point. I'm sure they'll be allowed to bring more pillows and blankets to make beds on the ground," Elma said.

"What if their jobs are important and they can't leave them," Argo asked.

"Don't be ridiculous, Argo. These jobs are just meant to keep us busy. There's no way that everyone is getting the bread you make every day. Half of it gets thrown out, I bet. It's just to get us exhausted by the end of the day so we don't act out." Argo sighed in response and ate her soup silently.

Elma started to speak again, "We can attempt to ask them about Kayo's family tomorrow, but tonight, we should just get some sleep. Well...I mean, you two should. You've probably never worked that hard before." The family finished up their dinner, and Kettle's parents and Elma took the dirty dishes upstairs to be cleaned. Kayo and Kettle had laid in their beds for sleep as they were instructed to do.

"Hey, Kettle," Kayo muttered. Kettle rolled over in his bed so he could look at her.

"Yeah?"

"I'm…I'm really sorry for being mean to you on Earth. You didn't have to help me yesterday and you did and… thank you for being a better person than me," she said. Kettle didn't quite know how to process this. He had helped her because she was so scared and alone— just like him, but she had also been the biggest bully in school. The apology meant a lot to him, but he didn't really know how to respond. His feelings of hatred and anger towards her for bullying him and his friends had disappeared the moment they landed on Eris and only had each other. He had no idea where the other kids went after they landed. He just hoped they had found their families and were safe.

"And for the record… I was jealous of how quickly you made your friends." Kayo rolled over and Kettle wasn't sure if she had fallen asleep or not.

"I would have been your friend too," he muttered. He wondered if she heard him, but it didn't appear so. Soon, he was deep in a dreamless sleep.

Morning rolled around far too quickly. Kettle's muscles ached from the day before. He rolled out of bed and rubbed his eyes.

"Remember, you don't talk to them until you guys know what to and not to say."

The Broken Kingdom of Orion

They were all upstairs before the sharp knocking started. Kojo opened the door to a smiling woman that looked exactly like Rose from the day before.

"Hello! My name is Roo. Isn't it a wonderful day to serve our gracious queen? Today, I am going to give you your food rations. How many people are working today?"

Kettle gasped but didn't say anything. He recognized the exact same movement and script that the previous girl, Rose, used. Elma suggested that they were people trained to follow a cookie-cutter form, but Kettle wasn't so sure.

"Actually, today we needed to make a request," Kojo started. Roo made a clicking noise, her head cocked to the side and she straightened up.

"You wish to make a request?" she asked with a big smile.

"Yes, our guest, Kayo, hasn't found her family. We need help on our small farm. We would like to request that the family be found and brought to help us on the farm. Our production for the queen would improve if we had the help. We are also requesting the day off from work to prepare our home for her family to move in." Roo stared at him for a moment. Her head tipped down and then straightened out.

"Your request has been approved on the grounds of faster production to serve our wonderful queen."

Kojo bowed his head in a show of gratitude. "Thank you."

"Your payment for this request is half rations today. Goodbye for today, and remember, the queen saved us all from the death of war," she continued. When she finished speaking, she turned on her heels and walked away. Kojo closed the door to the house and looked at his family.

Reji Ex

"Alright, we have work to do to get our sleeping quarters prepared for our new house guests." Kojo and Kettle left to take care of the animals for the day while Elma, Argo, and Kayo stayed back to rearrange the basement. Kayo and Elma hung up curtains between the beds in an attempt to give each person their privacy. Argo began redecorating and using some cheap paint on the walls to brighten the room.

"Why do you do that? We live in a basement." Argo groaned in irritation at Elma's question.

"Just because we live in a basement doesn't mean we can't try to make it homelike. Someday, things will go back to the way they once were and we won't have to live in the basement." Elma rolled her eyes but continued helping her sister decorate. "Besides, we want our new guests to feel welcomed here and not like they were moved to live in a basement." Kayo joined their conversation.

"I haven't seen my family in years. I hope they haven't changed."

"I'm sure they have. We all have in one way or another," Argo said. They finished hanging pictures and making the beds then made their way back upstairs. Kayo had noticed the house was empty when they first got there, but now, she really took in how defeated and sad the once happy home looked. The stone cabin was two stories tall at one time, but during the war, the family had deemed living upstairs unsafe and made their home in the basement for cover. Now, the top floor was full of empty rooms. The ground level was a barren open floor plan, showcasing what used to be a living room and the kitchen. The stove was no longer electric but a fireplace with a rack over the flames. The fireplace was also the only source of heat in the entire house. The kitchen cupboards were mostly full of food. Enough so that taking half portions wouldn't cause any worry today, but tomorrow would be a different question. A table with only four chairs sat in the center of the room, but other than that, the upstairs was empty. The simple, happy life that once lived here was hidden away underground.

    Kayo was pulled out of her thoughts by a timid knock on the door. It had to be her family. She excitedly jumped up and ran to answer the door.

Reji Ex

9: Battleship Juniper

Aries was still in his captain quarters when someone knocked loudly and frantically. He opened his eyes and groaned in irritation.

"What!" he demanded.

"Sir! A queen's ship has been spotted dead ahead," they shouted through the door. Aries rubbed his face as he sat up in his bed.

"How far away from Earth are we?"

"At least a day, sir," they answered. Aries got up, pulled his boots on, and started out the door.

"Go ahead and take out the ship. Don't kill anyone unless absolutely necessary," he ordered. The crewman saluted and ran to give the captain's orders to the others. Aries walked calmly to the kitchen, ignoring the frantic chaos around him. He trusted his crew and knew that they were more than capable of taking out a ship on their own without his constant instruction. Besides, if they weren't able to take on a ship then they weren't able to help him overthrow the queen.

Aries walked into the kitchen and poured himself a cup of coffee. He sipped his coffee in peace until Roman stumbled in.

The Broken Kingdom of Orion

"Good morning, Captain," he said with a mock salute. It had been a couple weeks since Aries had captured his ship and Roman asserted his role as "personal captain annoyer". This was a job he took very seriously. "Whatchya got there?" Roman asked.

"You know that tree that grows on Haumae? It somehow got to Earth and they made a drink out of it. It's called coffee. Some humans on my crew require it," Aries explained.

"Haumae? That's where that writer guy that wore that weird collar thing is from. That guy was a super bummer. He wrote a love story and everyone died. What's the point? If everyone dies, then why even write it?" Roman rambled.

"Is there something you need?" Aries asked.

"I'm just curious why you don't seem more excited to take out a ship. In fact, you don't seem to care at all. I thought you'd be looting with the others, at least," Roman said. Aries's eyes followed Roman as he walked around the kitchen looking for breakfast.

"I do not need possessions. They only weigh me down," Aries responded.

Roman smirked. "That is truly profound." Aries rolled his eyes. His hate-filled friendship with Roman was complicated. They tolerated each other. Roman respected Aries's cause of protecting the children, but what Aries would do after that would determine if he was worth Roman's time. Until then, they kindly irritated each other. Neither truly trusted the other and both knew this was a mutually beneficial engagement.

"And you? You're not with the others?" Aries questioned.

"I felt my time was better suited protecting the captain in case one of the queen's crew came in here to assassinate you," Roman joked. Aries looked at him over his cup of coffee.

Reji Ex

"You were a queen's man. Are you here to assassinate me?" Aries jibbed back.

Roman's joking manner quickly faded and his eyes darkened.

"Not before we save the children. I don't know about after that," he said in a serious tone that told Aries he was telling the truth. Aries nodded. He respected that answer.

A long time ago, Aries had been a father himself. He didn't come across many kids while destroying ships, but if he did, he was always sure to take care of them. Some kids he came across became crewmen, others left on pods to a planet of their choosing. But Aries had a rule—children's safety came first, and Roman seemed to have the same value.

Aries finished his cup of coffee and wandered the halls of his ship. Roman tagged along and annoyed him the whole time. After an hour or so, Aries looked out the window and saw the enemy ship was burning apart. He smiled as it burnt and waited for someone to find him to greet the new prisoners. They had a routine on his ship. It was mostly theatrics to instill fear into the enemy and create fearsome stories for anyone that might have heard of him. Everything was a massive illusion created by him and his crew.

Eventually, Aries started on his way to the prison cells. No one had come to get him; it shouldn't have taken this long. He decided that he would go down anyway. Roman, of course, followed along. They entered the prison and were met with all the crewmen that had looted the ship. All of the prisoners had their belongings with them. There were over a hundred prisoners packed into the cells. Aries looked around, confused.

"What's going on here?" he asked his crew. A woman stepped forward and pointed at him.

The Broken Kingdom of Orion

"It's the killer, Captain Aries!" she screamed. Aries rolled his eyes and pulled out his side arm and shot her in the face. A few prisoners screamed in fear but their fears were replaced with confusion when they saw sparks flickering from the bullet wound.

Aries walked over to the now dead woman and twisted her head off with ease. He held up the robot's head, its expression locked into one of surprise, and showed his crewmen.

"Kill anyone that looks like this. But be certain that it's a robot and not a person. I don't want unnecessary blood on my hands," he commanded. The crewmen nodded and began searching the groups for other robots. Aries walked over to one crewman.

"What is going on?" he demanded.

"We don't really know, Captain. We handcuffed a couple but then when we started questioning them…well…" the crewman gestured to one of the prisoners. Aries walked over to a terrified prisoner. He looked around for the brave one that was in every batch of prisoners they took, but there wasn't one. Every single person they had captured was terrified. Aries was confused by why the queen would recruit so many scared soldiers.

"Who are you people?" Aries asked the crowd.

"We're Kuiporians," one spoke up. Their voice was timid and scared; Aries almost missed it.

"Who are you? Why did you attack us?" another prisoner questioned.

"I'm Aries. You were on a queen's battleship. That's kind of my thing. Taking out her army," Aries explained.

"We just want to go home. We were on our way to Kuiper," someone said.

Reji Ex

"If you're Kuiporians then how are you on your way to Kuiper?" Aries pointed out.

"We're coming from a planet called Earth." Aries froze and looked at Roman.

"Hey, congrats, boss. You did it without even trying," Roman snarked.

"Captain, there were a couple injuries. Kuiporians can have a negative reaction to silver. Our handcuffs melted some of their skin," a crewman informed Aries. Aries rubbed the bridge of his nose.

"Okay, I want the kids to be taken care of. Feed them. People calm down when you feed them. Make sure they're coming from Earth and aren't secretly spies before you let them roam the ship freely." Aries walked out of the prison and made his way to the infirmary where Doc and Besnik were busy tending to burn wounds. Aries groaned in frustration at the mistake that had been made. He walked down the middle of the hospital beds.

"Okay, I am Captain Aries. This was a mistake. We thought you were a part of the queen's army. Your more silver tolerant friends told us that we, in fact, kidnapped and burnt a bunch of child refugees. That's not our intention, and once you're healed, we will be more than accommodating of your needs," Aries announced. Roman followed Aries but stopped when his eyes landed on one of the patients.

"It's you," he muttered. "I can't believe it's you!"

Roman rushed over to the patient and trapped him in a bone-crushing hug. The patient hugged back but hadn't said anything.

"I tried to find you. I never thought I would ever see you again," Roman told him. Aries walked over to the two to see what the commotion was about. Roman looked at Aries and smiled.

The Broken Kingdom of Orion

"Aries, this is my baby brother, Marko," Roman introduced him. Aries nodded.

"Hi," Marko said with a slight hand wave. Aries's eyes stopped and focused on Marko's wrist. A familiar bracelet hung from it, one that Aries hadn't seen in years.

"Where did you get that?" Aries asked, pointing to the bracelet. Marko looked at it. His eyes glazed over for a split second.

"It's my wife's bracelet. We were separated because she's not Kuiporian. She gave it to me to make me promise to come back for her— so we could be together," Marko said. Aries blinked.

"Your wife?"

"Yeah. Her name is Elenora."

"Wow, I can't believe I missed my baby brother's wedding," Roman teased. Aries took the bracelet off Marko's wrist.

"Hey!" he protested.

"I'm sorry. Is your wife one of the kids from Earth?" Aries asked.

"Yeah. Give me my bracelet back," Marko demanded.

"You won't need it. We're gonna be picking your wife up soon." Aries turned and walked out, leaving the two brothers to catch up. He went to the captain's deck to assure everyone that their destination was Earth and then made his way to his room. He sat at his desk, grinning at the bracelet in his hands. The engraving on the inside was Elenora's full name. He clicked on the activation button and the bracelet lit up. He smiled with joy.

"Elenora Lupa, I've finally found you."

Reji Ex

Marko and Roman were in the infirmary, catching up on their ten years away from each other.

"What was Earth like?" Roman asked. Marko shrugged.

"It wasn't that great. We had to go to school like children do, but we learned Earth stuff like who Christopher Columbus was."

"Who is he?"

"A bad guy that killed people, like Hitler."

"Who's Hitler?"

"Another bad guy that killed people."

Roman crossed his arms. "Earth doesn't sound like a fun place."

"Well, some of it is fun, like this city that El and I went to. It's called Vegas, and it was bright and loud. We saw a magician catch a lady on fire and the lady turned into a tiger," Marko rambled. Roman didn't quite care about the story but he was too ecstatic to have his brother again to stop him. Their mom and dad had been killed in the war, and Marko was the only family he had left. When he was told that Marko would be safe on Earth until after the war, he didn't risk it and sent him away. His hope of ever seeing him again was crushed when their planet turned into a rubble-filled ruin.

Marko yawned, and his eyes drooped a little.

"Are you tired? Maybe it's the medication making you sleepy," Roman suggested.

"Am I going to see her again?" Marko asked.

"If Aries said it then it must be true," Roman confirmed. Marko's eyes closed without another word. Roman watched him for a moment, then decided to leave and let his brother sleep. He would see him in the morning anyway. Roman made his way to his room. He passed a bunch of kids that he used to know from Kuiper. His smile couldn't fade. He finally felt like he was fixing something. The

The Broken Kingdom of Orion

children of his planet were grown and were here, alive. Aries brought his planet back to life.

Roman had joined the queen's army believing helping her cause was going to end the war sooner. He thought if he just helped her then there would be peace and he'd get his brother back. He no longer thought that way. When he saw his brother, his mind immediately realized what he had been doing for the queen— blowing up planets and killing billions of innocent lives. And here's Aries, reuniting him with his brother after only a couple of weeks. He had a change of heart but couldn't tell anyone. Now, he felt that his loyalty was owed to Aries. Besnik mentioned this feeling over breakfast one day, like a life debt was somehow owed to Aries. Roman finally understood what Besnik meant by that. Of course, he would never admit that to the captain.

Roman fell into his fluffy blankets and pulled out the pocket watch that had a baby picture of him and his brother glued to the cover. His brother was back in his life. This was perfect.

The next morning, Roman woke up. He started his day like normal by going to the kitchen to torment his captain. Aries was having his usual morning cup of coffee in the kitchen when Roman walked in. There was a dining hall that was just as fancy as the bedrooms, but Aries preferred to eat in the kitchen and sleep in a room the size of a broom closet. Roman didn't understand it completely, but Aries had told him that he didn't care too much about possessions. Aries looked up as he walked in and smiled. This caused Roman to stop in his tracks for a moment.

"Good morning," Aries greeted. Roman slowly walked over to get his own cup of coffee.

Reji Ex

"You seem uncharacteristically happy today," Roman pointed out.

"We will be on Earth in a few hours. The children will be saved," Aries said.

"A grown man shouldn't be happy about being near children," Roman teased.

Aries smirked at him and drank his coffee.

"According to the others, they're all adults now. Or at least teens. It doesn't matter. I think she's there."

"She? The queen?" Roman questioned.

"No…Just…" Aries smiled and giggled. Roman took a step back.

"You're scaring me," he said.

"Go talk to your brother. He's got a lot to tell you, I bet," Aries said. He got up and wandered away.

Roman took his advice and went to see his brother. Marko was deathly allergic to silver. Not every Kuiporian was, but when they were, it melted their skin. It was a common allergy among them. Roman was fortunate enough not to have the allergy, as Aries's handcuffs were all made out of silver. Marko had surface burns all over his torso and arms. Roman wondered if he fought to get them off or if he had chains along with the cuffs. Marko smiled weakly when Roman walked over to him.

"Hey, big bro," he greeted Roman.

"How are you feeling today?" Roman asked.

"It hurts to move," Marko muttered.

"Then don't move," Roman teased. Marko smirked and rolled his eyes.

"I did not miss your sarcastic jokes. Granted, I had a sarcastic friend named Kettle that picked up the slack."

The Broken Kingdom of Orion

"I'm glad you made friends. And you're married now?" Roman asked. Marko's face fell when he mentioned marriage. He missed his wife, and now that Aries took Elenora's bracelet, he felt even more distant from her.

"You're friends with that guy, right? The captain, I mean."

"Well, we're not really friends, but why?" Roman asked.

"He took my wife's bracelet from me. I was wondering if you could get it from him for me. I can't even move right now."

"I'll see if I can, but he seemed pretty certain that we were going to be on Earth today." Marko nodded and winced.

"Has Besnik seen you yet?" Roman asked.

"Yeah, he changed my bandages when I woke up and cleaned the burns, but there's not much he can do."

"What can I do for you right now that would help?" Roman asked. Marko opened his mouth to speak but ended up sighing instead. His eyes drifted away.

"I just want Elenora."

Roman gave a sympathetic smile at his hurting brother. He was both physically injured and heartbroken, and that was always a deadly combination. Roman didn't have this issue. He had never felt that way about anyone and didn't think it was in the cards for himself.

"Aries says he's getting her for you, and I choose to believe him. He hasn't lied to me yet," Roman said in an effort to comfort his brother.

"How long have you known him?" Marko asked.

"Not long, a month maybe."

"How can you be sure that he's not the guy that started all these wars?"

"Just a gut feeling. I…I helped the queen blow up a planet."

Reji Ex

Roman lowered his head in shame. Marko was too stunned to talk. He didn't know what to think or say. His brother had just admitted to genocide.

"Why would you do that?" Marko asked, bewildered.

"I was lied to. By her. They took over our planet and told us the kids we sent to Earth couldn't come back because of hostile planets in between us. I just wanted you back so we could be a family again."

"You killed people for me?" Marko asked. Horror was in his eyes as he looked at his brother, hoping for an answer that would ease him. Roman averted his eyes. The truth was, there was nothing he could say to make it sound good.

"You wouldn't understand. You were safe. We were forced to comply or else... There wasn't actually an 'or else'... we had to do what our queen commanded," he explained. Roman looked back at his brother before continuing. "But Aries isn't like her. He's her victim. He's the only surviving member of his planet. He doesn't kill without reason."

"You were a captain too?"

"Yes."

"Where's the rest of your crew?" Marko asked. Roman shook his head and looked away. Marko was asking a specific question and he knew it.

"The members of my crew that were willing to make a difference have joined Aries's crew," Roman said.

Marko nodded in understanding. "And the ones loyal to the queen were killed for their loyalty." our

"They saw how well he treated the ones who surrendered and chose to die."

"Aries killed them," Marko stated.

"They were given the choice to live or remain loyal and they chose—"

"Aries killed them!" Marko snapped.

"Yes! Yes, they are dead. They're gone. They fought a war that they were lied to about, and they died because they wanted to stay loyal," Roman snapped back.

Marko and Roman looked at each other without speaking. In their silence, Roman's shoulders began to ease. He hadn't even noticed that he tensed up, but he must have. He looked around at the other patients that were watching the small screaming match, but they averted their eyes when Roman saw them. Roman cleared his throat as if to clear the awkwardness from the air.

"Aries is going to get your wife from Earth. Isn't that good?" Roman asked.

"Why? What does he want with her?" Marko questioned. Roman looked out the window and his eyes widened. Marko followed his gaze, fighting against the pain to see what his brother was looking at. He smirked and leaned back in his bed. "I guess we're gonna find out soon enough. Welcome to Earth, Roman," Marko said.

Roman was amazed by how big Earth was. Kuiper was a dwarf planet and only a fraction of the size of the giant before him. The blue portions of Earth, water, covered most of it, unlike any other planet he's seen so far. Earth was special; Roman could see that. He didn't know how to describe it, but there was something about planet Earth that drew Roman to it. Just looking at it from a safe distance made Roman smile in amazement. Earth was the planet of fairy tales.

10: Earth

Elenora slammed open the doors as she stormed into The General's office. A soldier chased her in protest but was unable to stop her from entering.

"I'm sorry, General. I was unable to stop her," he apologized.

"That's okay, Private." The General turned his attention to the person sitting in front of him. "Mr. President, I would like you to meet one of the residents here who's going through the human training. Her name is Elenora." The man swiveled around in the chair to look at Elenora, and sure enough, it was the President of the United states. Elenora was taken aback for a moment. The president stood up and shook Elenora's hand.

"Pleased to meet you," he said.

"Mr. President, I...I didn't know you were here."

"Yes, well, we like to keep the president's location on the down low, Elenora," The General responded. The president waved his hand in dismissal.

"No matter. We were just finishing up our business. You seem like you have something important to discuss with the General." Elenora got flustered and said the first thing that she could think of.

The Broken Kingdom of Orion

"I like Hamliton the musical," she stammered, as if a musical about past presidents would help in this current situation.

"'Course you do. Everyone does," he said politely. He nodded at The General before walking out. When the door closed behind him, Elenora sat down and gasped.

"That was the president!"

"Yes, it was, Elenora. What do you need?" Elenora shook her head to clear out the starstruck and pulled out the photo from her birthday that Marko had left for her.

"I need you to explain this," she said. The General took the photo and looked at it, then looked back up at Elenora.

"This is you," he said. Elenora rolled her eyes and pointed to the guy in the background. The General squinted at the image to get a closer look.

"That's interesting. I know this man."

"Who is he?" she asked.

"Well, I can't tell you that. There is such a thing as anonymity. Besides, he's not supposed to be on Earth anymore."

"Wait! Marko said he was following me. Is he the person that brought me to Earth? Is he my father?"

"Marko talked to him? That's against the rules, Elenora."

"I didn't know till the day he left that he talked to another alien." The General groaned in frustration. He took rules very seriously, but he couldn't punish someone that was no longer on the planet.

"Elenora, I assure you that the man in the picture is not your father. He's Kuiporian and you're…you're not. But that's all I'm telling you." He stood up in his chair and started to walk away.

"Where are you going?" Elenora asked.

Reji Ex

"I have to go to apprehend him. He's not supposed to be on Earth," he said.

Elenora got up and followed him out the door.

"Why isn't he supposed to be on Earth?"

"He committed a crime on Earth and was ordered to leave," The General explained. The General went into a room, but when Elenora tried to follow him, she was stopped by two army men. Elenora looked at them before deciding to pout and walk away. She walked back to The General's office and was stopped again before going in.

"You don't have clearances to be in there alone," the guard said. Elenora looked at him with fake surprise.

"Oh! The General had to leave quickly and told me to wait for him to come back. It was something dealing with the president. I don't know," she lied. The guard nodded and stood aside. Elenora entered the office and quickly, but quietly, began rummaging through the files that were on the wall. She rapidly looked for her own file while keeping an ear out for anyone coming. While she searched, she realized the files were organized by planet. She rolled her eyes. She wouldn't be able to find her own file because she doesn't have a planet that she knows of. She flicked through folders divided by planet and counted. She noticed that the only planets listed were from the Milky Way Galaxy.

It didn't mean much to her, but it was an observation. Perhaps other galaxies had their own Earth-like child protective planets. She didn't know nor did she care. She kept looking for her own folder. After thirty minutes of searching, she became helpless. She slumped into the guest chair to think about where her folder might be hidden. Then, she got an idea.

The Broken Kingdom of Orion

Elenora quietly walked around the desk and sat in The General's chair, slowly pulling out a drawer so it wouldn't make any noise. She looked through the contents of the drawer and then slowly closed it when she didn't find what she was looking for. She found her file in the bottom drawer on the right side of the desk. She pulled it out, plopped it right on the desk, and began reading it. What was written were words that chilled her blood.

Planet: Orion (nebulized for unknown reasons). Her planet was gone. She was probably the last one from her planet and never even knew it. She didn't feel the need to read anymore. She put the folder back in the desk and started to walk out the door. She walked out of the main building and went back to her empty house.

Meanwhile, Aries had landed his escape pod in the middle of the Nevada desert. He hadn't wanted to take a big crew. Even the crew he did take wasn't making him too happy. He brought Besnik for medical reasons, leaving Doc behind to care for the injured Kuiporian children. He was more experienced and the kids needed his practiced hand.

He also brought Roman, because Marko asked that Roman bring his wife back to him safely. Aries rolled his eyes but honored that request. Aries believed that young love was dumb. It was what got his planct blown up, after all. The trio began their hike through the desert.

"Where are we going?" Roman asked.

"I don't know," Aries answered.

"Do we have a plan?" Besnik asked. Aries shrugged. "I don't like that plan."

Reji Ex

"Well, it could be worse. We could be on an unfamiliar planet with a giant star that melts skin blaring down on us…oh wait," Roman teased.

"They call that star 'the sun'. And it gives food to plants," Besnik informed them.

"How does it do that if it's in the sky?" Roman asked.

"The plant absorbs the light." Besniks answer confused Roman.

"Does it absorb the light? Then there wouldn't be light left!"

"It's called photo-something-sis, and it's a real thing."

"Photo-somehting-sis? That doesn't even make sense."

Aries turned on the two bantering males. "Can you two shut the fuck up?"

"Do you think plants absorb the sun, Aries?" Roman asked.

"I don't care. Look, there's a town ahead. We can ask locals about the children's camp. They should know about it. Right?" The three of them walked towards the town. When they approached, Aries's eyes locked on a local. He stopped in his tracks and watched the man.

"Why are we stopping?" Roman asked. Aries silently followed the man as he slipped into a restaurant. The two followed him. When they entered the restaurant, the man was seated at a table. Aries quickly sat at the table in front of the man. The other two followed and sat down as well. The man jumped when they sat in front of him.

"Aries? Do you know this man?" Roman asked. Aries just glared at the man across from him. Aries and the man stared at each other for a moment before the man looked at Besnik and Roman.

"Did you just call him Aries?" he asked.

"That's the alias he's going by," Besnik said.

"Is that not his name?" Roman asked. Aries looked at Besnik in surprise.

The Broken Kingdom of Orion

"I figured it out," Besnik said.

"Figured out what?" Roman asked.

"That this isn't just a man named Aries. This is Lord Dante Lupa, King of Orion," the man said.

Roman looked between the three men in front of him with confusion before leaning back in his chair, content enough to not need any more answers.

"I have been a loyal advisor for years," the man said.

"To my wife, actually, Jovian" Aries corrected.

"Okay, yes…yes, I admit it. I was working for her the entire time. But when I came to you and told you what was really happening you laughed me out of the room," Jovian complained. Suddenly, their conversation was stopped when a waitress came by to get their drink orders. The waitress went to get their drinks while the men looked at the menus.

"So where are you from, mysterious man that's my captain's enemy," Roman asked. The man looked up at him. He cleared his throat awkwardly.

"I'm Kuiporian originally, but…I moved to Helix to work for the royal family and assisted their arranged marriage on Orion," Jovian said.

"It wasn't arranged," Aries said from behind his menu.

"How long have you been on Earth?" Roman asked. Aries slammed his menu down and looked between the man and Roman.

"He's been here for 21 years. Right?" Accusation tinged Aries' voice.

"I think I'll have the chicken tenders and french fries," Besnik said nervously.

Reji Ex

"Great choice, great choice...what is it?" Roman said sarcastically.

"It's like pollo on Kuiper," Jovian said.

"Oh! Then yeah, me too," Roman agreed. The waitress came back with their drinks and took their food orders.

"Helix has been nebulized," Besnik said.

"When?" Jovian asked.

"Recently. Roman here led a raid on the planet that ended in it being blown up," Besnik explained.

"Hi, I'm Roman. My loyalty was very flimsy but I feel pretty solid about Aries even though he hates me. Aries found my kid brother."

"I hate you because your loyalty is flimsy," Aries said. Roman laughed.

"So, what brings you to Earth?" the man asked. Aries held up the bracelet that he snatched from Marko. Jovian's eyes widened for a moment but then he nodded.

"She is here."

"Who is?" Roman asked.

"I'll tell you in a second. I want him to tell me one thing first. Why did you take her?" Aries asked the man. Jovian scoffed.

"I told you there was someone coming to destroy the planet and you laughed me out of the room," he said.

"You told me there was an enemy. We were a peaceful planet with no enemies. You sounded like a lunatic."

"Yeah, now you're one man with a thousand enemies," he replied.

"He has allies," Roman protested.

The Broken Kingdom of Orion

"I took her because I didn't want the entire race destroyed. I wanted there to be at least one Orion left." The waitress brought their food and the group began eating.

"Oh my god! This is amazing!" Besnik praised.

"How did you survive?" the man asked. The men all stopped eating and turned to Aries. Aries looked at them unsure of what to really say.

"I don't know. I can't honestly tell you. I was in the nursery during the explosion," Aries explained.

"Why did you have a nursery? That's pretty weird. Right? Unless you…" Roman started but then the realization hit him. "Oh. Is…is my brother's wife…?"

"I don't know, but we're gonna find out," Aries said. Roman gasped.

"Is that why you're such a big meany head? Because you're all heartbroken inside and everything. Aries, I had no idea that your back story was so tragic."

"And we all have this guy to thank for that," Aries said pointing to Jovian.

"No, we have your wife to thank, actually," he replied.

"That's fair. Every bad thing in the galaxy is happening because of her," Besnik added. Jovian looked past them to the door of the restaurant then quickly dipped under the table.

"What's happening? Is this an Earth thing?" Roman asked.

"Umm…it is when there's a bunch of Army men that just came in and are probably here to arrest you," Jovian said from under the table.

"This is a setup," Besnik said.

Reji Ex

"It's not a setup. He had no idea we were coming in order to set this up. Just eat your chicken and act natural," Aries instructed in a hushed voice.

"I literally don't know how to act naturally here. This is not my planet," Roman whispered back. Aries slowly turned around so he could see the group of Army men that were in the restaurant. There was an obvious leader talking to the waitress that was serving them. Aries couldn't tell what they were saying, but she definitely pointed to their table. Aries turned back around and continued eating.

"I think we might be in trouble, guys. The waitress just pointed at us."

"I literally cannot act natural," Roman harshly whispered.

"You lead a mission to blow up a planet and you can't lie to a couple of Earthlings?" Aries asked. The leader of the group came over to their table.

"Hello, gentlemen. We're looking for a suspicious character. He looks like the man in the background of this picture," he said, handing Aries the picture. Aries took the picture and looked at it. The man he was talking to was in the background, but in the foreground of the picture was a young woman with his blue hair and his silver eyes. She was smiling in front of a birthday cake. He looked at the picture and felt like he's known her his entire life. He stood up and looked at The General.

"Where did you get this picture?" he asked.

"That's classified information, sir," The General said.

"Where's this girl?"

"Classified, sir."

The Broken Kingdom of Orion

"No, this is my daughter. I've spent 20 years looking for her. Where is she?" Aries demanded. The General looked back at his men, then back at Aries.

"This is all classified information, sir. I cannot disclose this information to you. But if you come with us, we can talk about this at a disclosed location."

"We all know that you mean Area 51. You're doing tests on aliens there and we're gonna set them free someday!" a patron with an "I love Aliens" t-shirt shouted to them. Aries gave the patron a weird look.

"We should…we should go. Alien enthusiasts get really weird," The General instructed. Aries and his group stood up and followed The General out of the restaurant.

"You can't hide the truth from us forever, government drone!" the patron shouted.

"This planet is weird," Besnik whispered. The three men were loaded into the back of a military vehicle. Army men with guns sat next to them in a silent, menacing manner. Aries's heart raced, but he kept quiet. Besnik and Roman chatted idly and nervously in the otherwise silent car ride.

"I've got to be honest. I did not expect Aries to sell us out like that," Roman said.

"Yeah, what was that back there? We were going undetected," Besnik said.

"He's right. Alien enthusiasts dye their hair crazy colors. We would have never known you were aliens until you said you were El's father," one soldier said.

"Um, we don't use the A word. They're people from different planets," another soldier corrected.

"You can't talk about El. That's classified information."

"Oh, come on. How classified can it be? He's her father," the first one protested.

"He could be lying to get classified info. That's why it's classified!"

Suddenly the soldiers were all arguing with one another until the vehicle stopped. The General opened the back of the vehicle and sighed in frustration, seeing his men arguing with each other. Aries, Besnik, and Roman exited the vehicle.

"Did you do this?" The General asked Aries.

"Did he...cause them to fight?" Roman questioned. The General rolled his eyes and turned around.

"Forget it. Come with me." The group started walking but Aries stopped short. He looked across the lot and saw her. She was looking at them and started walking toward them.

"That's the girl in the picture," Roman said. The General stopped when he heard Roman say that and looked. Elenora was walking up to them. The General was saddened, knowing that he couldn't keep her from her real father. He looked down for a moment before deciding he had to let her go.

"Elenora, we believe this might be your real father," he told her. Aries gave a slight smile. Elenora gave a nervous smile back.

"You're the guy?" she asked. Aries chuckled.

"I'm the guy," he said, nervously.

"I don't think I've ever seen him smile before," Besnik whispered to Roman.

"I have. Once, at breakfast. It was as weird as this," Roman whispered back.

The Broken Kingdom of Orion

"We still need to verify everything though. So, maybe he's not," The General said.

He said this because it was protocol, but the truth was, Elenora was a female version of Aries; long blue hair, silver eyes, pale skin. The General led Aries away from Elenora.

11: Eris

Kayo spent the majority of the day in bed crying. The two families didn't bother her and let her cry. She hadn't seen her brother or father in years. Hearing about their death was traumatizing. Her mother and sister were the only ones that came when her family moved in. The others were dead from war. She was heartbroken. She'd never see her brother or father again. At the end of the day her mother, Tovah, and her sister, Amita, came down to check up on her. They sat next to her on her bed and held her.

"I've got to say, this is easier than our other job," Amita said. Kayo smiled slightly and leaned against her sister.

"We're glad we have you back, Kayo. We know how hard this must be for you," her mother soothed.

"But it's nice to have a place where we can say 'that stupid queen started this war and killed our father and brother' without worrying that one of her stupid drones will kill us," Amita said. Kayo sat up and wiped her tears away.

"We have to do something," she said.

"Well, there's nothing we can do," Tovah said. Kayo shook her head and rummaged through her bag.

The Broken Kingdom of Orion

"On Earth, we learned about a country that overthrew its government. We can start a revolution," she proposed. She took a book out of her bag and handed it to her mother. "Just read about it. It's all real. People snuck around, faked alliances, there was a war and everything."

"War is what got us here, Kayo. We don't want more war," Tovah stated.

"No, we want freedom and revenge for what the queen did," Kayo said. "Just read the book. Okay?"

"I don't have to. I'm in," Amita said.

"No! This, just talking about this, is dangerous," Tovah argued. Kettle's family came down the stairs at that moment with dinner.

"Is everything alright?" Argo asked.

"Everything is fine, thank you," Tovah said.

"We're debating whether we can start a revolution or not," Amita said. Argo gasped in shock. It was silent for a moment. No one knew what to say. No one was openly admitting that they agreed to this, but no one denied it either.

"We're the only bread bakers in town," Elma said. "So what?"

"So, what if paper accidentally got into the bread that gets sent to everyone in town? What if everyone met in one underground location secretly? Hear what the rest of the town has to say about it?" Elma said.

"This is so risky and the risk is our lives!" Tovah said.

Argo eyed Elma. "You said that too quickly, Elma. You've been thinking about this before." Elma shrugged and ate her dinner.

"I mean, we all have," Kojo said.

"Kojo!" Argo scolded.

Reji Ex

"No, I mean it. There's more of us than them. We can start an uprising. We can overthrow the hold the queen has on us. At least in our small town. Once we liberate ourselves, we can save the rest of the planet." Argo shook her head.

"We can at least invite everyone. What's the worst that can happen?" Kayo asked.

"The worst that can happen is someone snitches and we all get killed. I say no," Tovah said.

"Oh, we're voting? Are we gonna honor everyone's vote? I vote yes," Elma said.

"I vote yes," Amita agreed.

"Five yesses," Kojo pointed out. Everyone looked to Kettle.

"People will die regardless," Kettle said. He looked up at his family surrounding him. His mother sighed in despair.

"Alright, then. What's the plan?" Argo asked the group.

"Well, we can sneak a message to everyone with paper inside the bread," Elma said.

"Where are we going to get that much paper?" Tovah asked.

"I actually have a ream of paper in my bag!" Kayo said. She retrieved the paper out of her bag and a couple of pens.

"Where did you get all this?" her mother asked.

"We were allowed to bring things from Earth. I brought a bunch of art supplies, and paper, and books I liked," she explained.

"Okay, everyone grab a pen and start writing," Elma said.

"Write what?" Kojo asked.

"Write...town meeting, basement of...basement of where?" Elma asked.

"Oh! The old school! It's big enough, and it's abandoned," Amita said.

The Broken Kingdom of Orion

"Okay, town meeting in the basement of the old school at 2100. Let's start this very illegal thing that will get us killed if we fail," Tovah said sarcastically.

"But if we don't fail, then we've freed a planet," Elma said. The families got to work and spent a good portion of the night writing notes for the village.

The next day, they worked as if they hadn't planned anything. They fed and cleaned the animals in the barns. Then they washed up and started assisting with baking, planting the notes in the bread. The bread was baked and then the queen's assistants came to clear out the inventory and left. The family quietly went about their lives as if they hadn't committed a crime. In fact, they didn't say anything to each other for the rest of the night. They silently did their jobs like normal the next day. The assistants came and took their hard days work, as usual. Then, they started walking to town.

Town wasn't too far away from the stone cabin, but the trip would have been easier if they were allowed cars or even horse and buggy. The families were exhausted from working all day. They didn't want to hike to town, but most of them felt that they didn't have a choice. They got to the old school as the rest of the town was arriving. Tovah was amazed, it seemed like everyone was there and hadn't ignored the notes. Everyone queued into the room as quietly as possible and sat on the floor. Some stood around the walls. Everyone was quiet so as to not get caught. When it seemed like no one else was coming, the doors were closed, and Kettle and Kayo's families stood before them.

"Hello, friends, neighbors," Amita started.

Reji Ex

"Let's get to the chase. Who wants to live their lives like this?" Elma cut her off, taking charge. To no surprise, the townspeople looked around but no one raised their hands.

"We have an idea, but it's dangerous. If you aren't willing to risk your life to free yourselves, you're free to go. We can't stop you," Elma said. A few people started to leave but when they noticed that their families weren't coming with them, they started to argue instead. Everyone began to argue. Some were starting to yell how this was all dangerous, even meeting like this. Some were arguing that they were waiting for a sign and this was it. Kettle's family looked at each other helplessly. Kayo whistled loudly to get the attention of the fighting townspeople.

"I...Guys, you sent us to a planet that was entirely built on revolution. I mean, the country we were placed in was still revolting when we left!"

"Can someone explain what's happening?" an Erisian shouted.

"We want to start a revolution. The kids have been learning about it on Earth and it applies here," Elma said.

"If we band together, plan together, then we have a real chance of freeing our town," Amita added.

"When our town is free, we can move on to the next town. We can slowly free the planet. Not only that, but when we relieve the next town over— we'll gain more fighters," Kojo said.

"We just got out of a war. You want us to go back to one?" someone shouted.

"If you want to continue working in the mines every day with no break that's fine, but we just ask you not to get in our way," Kojo replied.

The Broken Kingdom of Orion

"Who wants to free our town?" Amita asked. The townspeople looked at each other, daring those around them to raise their hand first.

"I don't like it here," Kayo said. "On Earth, we had to stay in a military camp, but that camp was set up to give us the illusion of living on Earth. There were stores and restaurants. We were even allowed to openly insult the guy running the place and, let me tell you, he held favoritism to Kettle's friend."

"That's true," Kettle said.

"We weren't worried about our safety if we didn't follow the rules to a T. We were allowed to move around the camp freely and live our lives. When we were tired, we didn't need permission to take breaks, we just went to our dorms and took a nap. We weren't threatened with our children's safety," Kayo continued. She paused and looked around. She noticed something that she never thought to think of. She noticed that there weren't new people in town. There weren't kids that hadn't been on Earth. Nobody had children after the war. She knew this was because of the queen somehow. She looked at her sister.

"Kayo has a book about the American Revolution. We can pass it around town to whoever wants to read it. It's about a small country that took on a powerhouse army and won. It's true even! We can use it as a guide or motivation," Amita said.

"Why did they do it? Were they successful?" someone from the crowd asked.

"Yes, they were successful. And they inspired another country to do the same,"

Kettle said. The crowd muttered amongst themselves for a moment.

"What do we honestly have to lose? Life? We've lost that already," someone shouted. A couple of people agreed.

"Pros and cons. Pros: we have our lives back. Cons: we die," someone said.

"Pros: Our children can have the life they deserve. Cons: we have to fight a little longer than we wanted," another answered.

"The queen took our children to manipulate us into submission. What do you think she's gonna do when we aren't submissive anymore?"

"Nothing! Because we outnumber her freaking goonies!" someone shouted from the back of the crowd.

"Hey! I have a question. Has anyone else noticed something weird about those girls?" Kettle yelled over the arguing crowd.

"They all look the same."

"They say the same thing every day."

"We never see them unless we say something unfounded or when they collect what we've mined."

"Doesn't anyone find that weird?" Kettle asked.

"What are you talking about, son?" Kojo asked.

"Everyone! Let's meet back here tomorrow, same time. I have a theory I want to test out. If I'm right, it might change your minds," Kettle announced. With that, everyone mumbled to each other and went out into their world. They went home as silently as they had come.

There was a long walk for the family to get back to their farm, but as soon as they did, they collapsed in their beds to go to sleep.

"Kettle," Argo said.

"Yes?" he replied.

"What exactly is your idea?" she asked him.

"I...I don't think you'll be happy about it, but...I think I'm gonna kill one of the assistants," he said. She gasped.

"Kettle, you can't kill anyone."

"That's the thing...I don't think they're people," he said softly.

"You know, so what if he does? I mean, we're gonna go to war. Might as well get used to killing now," his dad said.

"I don't feel comfortable with this," Argo said. "What if she is a person and you murder her? You're prepared for that consequence?"

"Well, yeah. This is war we're going into," Kettle said.

"I can do it! I want to kill," Elma said.

"Me too," Amita replied.

"Tomorrow, only one assistant will come by. We can kill her and no one will know about it. If she's a person, we'll bury her in the yard somewhere," Kettle said. His mother groaned loudly.

"You've already planned this all out?" she complained.

"Let's try to get some sleep, guys. Either way, we still have a mountain of chores to do tomorrow," Tovah said. Everyone agreed and attempted a peaceful sleep but that didn't seem possible. There was too much at stake.

The next morning, everyone rolled out of bed and started their day. Tovah and Argo began making breakfast when the anticipated knock on the door arrived. Kettle slipped a kitchen knife into his sleeve and Argo looked at her son nervously. There was a second knock. Kojo opened the door. The assistant entered with her traditional smile.

"You were late to respond. To honor the queen properly we ask that you open your door on the first knock," she said.

"I understand. We were just starting breakfast, that's all," Kojo replied. Kettle snuck up behind the assistant while she and Kojo had their normal conversation. While the assistant wasn't looking, he plunged the knife deep into her back. He yelped as a shock rippled through him. The assistant fell to the floor in seizure-like movements.

"The queen would like to speak to you. We worship our loving queen. We live in a peaceful-peaceful-peaceful…the queen protects us," she spat out before her eyes dimmed. She stopped jerking around and the color in her eyes turned all white. Kettle carefully pulled the knife out of her back. He kneeled beside her and sliced from the base of the neck to mid-back, pulling the skin away. Everyone in the room was too stunned to say anything.

"I knew it. She…she's a robot. They're all robots," he whispered. Kojo slammed the door shut and locked it.

"Quickly, take her to the basement and dismantle her. We don't know if she's bugged or if she'll wake up," he instructed. Kayo and Kettle dragged the body of the assistant to the basement. They took turns using the knife to mutilate the body into pieces. Kettle pointed to a machine piece that was charred like it was on fire.

"Look! The knife must have shortened her circuit. That's what killed her, I think." Kayo looked at the pieces strewn across the floor. "I bet we can study this and figure out an accurate way to shut them all down. Or what they even do."

The robot was ripped to pieces and left lying on the ground while Kayo and Kettle made their way to the barns to start their work.

12: Earth

Upon interrogation, Aries explained to The General how Queen Nava was organizing the arrival of children on Earth and how she was the one picking them up when they grew up. They brainstormed together, trying to figure out why she would be collecting children off of planets and blowing up a few of them but not all of them. They couldn't think of a reason, but Aries explained how the planet Orion was the first victim of her dastardly plans. Queen Nava started this war for no apparent reason, and Aries was planning on stopping her.

    The General gave Aries directions to Elenora's house. Aries made his way to meet his daughter, for real this time. The General spoke with Besnik and Roman before escorting them back to the ship just out of the Earth's atmosphere. Aries walked up the steps to Elenora's front door and took a deep breath before knocking. She opened the door with a smile.

    "Hi," she said. He smiled back.

Reji Ex

"Hi! We met earlier but, umm…I'm Aries, actually Dante…no, no, you can call me Aries— or dad, if you want," he rambled, trying to introduce himself. Elenora smiled wider.

"I'll call you Aries for now."

Aries nodded in understanding and they went inside. Elenora started to make tea for them while Aries sat at her kitchen table. He felt awkward and it wasn't a feeling that he had often or enjoyed. He didn't know what to say to her or how to even start a conversation.

"So…" he started but was stopped by the lack of words to continue. Elenora handed him his cup of tea and he sipped it. "This is really good! Did you make it yourself?"

"It's a tea bag. You just put it in hot water. The British make whole pots of it with loose leaves, but Americans don't have time for that. Plus, they threw it in the harbor. I think the government secretly doesn't trust the masses with loose leaves anymore," Elenora said. Aries nodded, but truthfully, he didn't understand what she was talking about. They were planets apart and he hated it.

"Did you abandon me?" Elenora asked. Aries' eyes widened.

"What? No, of course not. You were kidnapped by one of your mother's goons." Aries sighed and looked at his cup of tea. "I…I thought you were dead for years. I hated her for killing you."

"The file said I was from Orion. That's not a planet," Elenora said. Aries fidgeted. He suspected that these hard subjects would come up, but he wasn't prepared at all. His hands trembled as he grabbed his cup of tea and drank it to calm his nerves.

"It's no longer a planet," he stated.

"Why?"

Aries tapped his fingers against the table. He wondered why he was so nervous and scared talking to Elenora. He wasn't this nervous

The Broken Kingdom of Orion

for The General or anyone he's ever met, for that matter. He looked up at his daughter and noticed her shifting her weight between her feet. He smiled gently at her.

"Why don't you sit down?" he suggested. As she slowly sat in a chair across from him, her nerves began to ease and Aries breathed in relief. Her nervousness had been projecting onto him. This was a skill she did not know how to control yet.

"This isn't an easy story for me to talk about, and with you being nervous, I get nervous," Aries said.

"I always dreamed that you'd come for me, but I've been here so long that I eventually gave up on it. I figured I was unwanted and dropped off," Elenora said. Aries laughed. She looked at him in surprise.

"When you were born the whole planet rejoiced and celebrated for days," Aries said. Elenora scoffed and rolled her eyes but smiled at him.

"And, pray tell, why would a whole planet be happy that I was born?" Her words were tainted with sarcasm.

Aries blinked at her reaction.

"Because…because you're the princess of Orion. My daughter. I know some places were more excited for male heirs but Orion wasn't discriminatory of gender," Aries said. Elenora stood up suddenly. "Is everything okay?"

"I don't…I don't understand. Princess? Then what happened? Orion isn't even a planet. It's a nebula. You know, a giant ball of gas. And you said my mother's goons stole me. Why would the queen do that? I don't understand. This doesn't make any sense," Elenora ranted as she paced the floor. Aries stood up and put his hands on her shoulders to calm her.

Reji Ex

"Look, I want, more than anything, to say something that would comfort you. To tell you the answers to all of your questions. But I don't have the answers. And this story doesn't comfort me either. Truth is, I was really, truly, deeply in love with your mother. She meant the world to me, and I thought I mattered to her too. One day she just…snapped. She was building a bomb in secret that I didn't know about. I ran to the nursery to get you instead of leaving with her. When I got there, you were gone. I had only seconds left after that. I thought…I don't know. I thought she had you. After I escaped I got a message saying you weren't with her. I never knew exactly who took you. I never thought I'd see you again." Aries smiled to himself. He was overjoyed to have his little girl back, even if it meant having this complicated discussion.

"She blew up the planet?" she asked.

"Yes. Yeah, she did. I don't know if anyone else survived. I like to believe that they did and just found new planets that would let them live in peace. Orion was a peaceful planet. There wasn't any of this theft, or killing, or wars. This was a violent lifestyle adjustment for me," Aries said.

"So now what? You found me, are you just gonna leave me again?" she asked.

"Look, the General is currently giving out a statement to the other people here. They are going to…do training to go out and live their lives on Earth like Earth people," Aries said. Elenora nodded.

"Yeah, the training. I know about it. I begged to join the program." Aries studied Elenora's features. She was definently Orion. She had none of Nava's features but for all he knew Elenora wasn't actually his but some other Orian's kid. It didn't matter to him if that was true or not. Worst case scenario, he took care of a dead friend's kid. Best case, he's the father. Both resulted in Aries being Elenora's caretaker and father figure.

"Here's the deal. You don't know me, and you don't know any life other than one on Earth. If you want to stay here, then I understand. I can't promise that I'll return though because…there's unfinished business. If you want to come with me then that's great, but I know it's a lot of change all at once," Aries said.

"If you're able to come back, will you?"

"I would, for you. Yes, of course. But space is big and your mother sends assassins regularly to remind me of our wedding vows of death being the only reason to part."

"I got married. My marriage is a happy one though."

"He seems like a nice guy," Aries muttered. Elenora stared at him.

"You know him?"

"Yeah, that's something I had to disclose to The General. Kuiporians are coming back and I've been tasked with picking up the Erisians too."

"You have my husband with you?"

"Yes, he's staying on my ship because his brother is a part of my crew," Aries explained.

"I'm coming too," Elenora stated. She went to her bedroom and began packing a bag of her clothes.

Aries raised his voice so Elenora could still hear him, "Why? To be with Marko? There's a war going on. You shouldn't make a decision based on love alone."

"I'm not! My father's gonna be there. My husband's gonna be there. And in the meantime, I can save the galaxy. It's a smart choice, really," Elenora responded. She flung her bag over her shoulder and looked at Aries to lead the way. Aries shrugged and walked out. Elenora followed behind him.

"Oh, this is yours by the way," he said, handing her the bracelet. "It was a gift from the whole kingdom when you were a baby. I'm surprised you still have it."

Jax and Vine approached, interrupting them. "We heard you were leaving," Vine said.

"Yeah, this is my father, Aries. Aries, these are my friends, Jax and Vine."

"We're planning on moving to not Nevada!" Vine said cheerfully.

"So, this is where we part ways?" Elenora asked.

"Well, unless we can come with you?" Jax asked. The three looked back at Aries.

"Oh no, I'm not kidnapping a bunch of Earth kids," he protested.

"We're not from Earth," Jax argued.

"And we're not kids either. I'm 25," Vine added. "We can go with you if you let us."

"Hey, I haven't seen my daughter in 21 years and was really hoping this would be a father-daughter, catch-up while saving the galaxy trip," Aries said.

"Well, we could be a part of your crew. Right? You'll never see us," Jax suggested. Aries studied Jax for a moment before slowly nodding in agreement. He wondered how Jax would know that but decided he had possibly heard the rumors that he carefully set up around the galaxy.

"Yay! This will be the ultimate road trip," Vine cheered.

"Without a road," laughed Elenora. The four made their way to the launch pad where they would take a shuttle to the Battleship Juniper. Elenora sat in a window seat, excited to finally see what

The Broken Kingdom of Orion

space is like. She was the only one of her friends to have never seen space despite being from the planet Orion.

Before the shuttle was able to take off, The General came down the rows of seats. He stopped at Elenora.

"I wanted you to have this," he said. He handed her the necklace that he gave her for her birthday.

"I was already given this."

"I know, but you were going to leave it. It's a homing device for anywhere in the Milkyway. Just press the gem in the middle and Earth soldiers will come find you," he explained. Elenora hugged her pseudo-dad. As a military man, he was unable to show his emotions well, but he showed his love with gifts and service. Aries got out of his seat and held his hand out to The General.

"Sir, thank you for raising my daughter," he said solemnly. The General shook his hand firmly.

"Just take care of her. And bring her to visit me, if you can."

Aries nodded in agreement and The General turned to get off the shuttle. As the shuttle broke out of the atmosphere of Earth, Elenora looked back at Aries.

"How long until we're on your ship?" she asked.

"Not that long. Maybe an hour."

"Can you tell me about Orion while we wait?"

Aries looked at her stone-faced but nodded. He spoke of the planet as if they were still on it, in such vivid detail that she felt like she had seen it herself.

Orion, a long time ago

Reji Ex

Young Dante was ten years old when his father, the King, had told him about the first royal test. His father told him that this was a royal test that every prince or princess had to do in order to rule over Orion. They don't let anyone who failed this test stay in the palace. His father said that so far, no royal member had ever failed this test. Dante was worried that he would be the first.

The test was really simple. The prince was ordered to go to the top of the mountain and retrieve an egg from the nest of an iridescent zilu bird without injuring it in any way. The zilu bird makes its nest on the mountaintop, at the very top of a fluff tree. Dante was halfway through the fluff tree forest when the terrain started to incline. The mountain itself was not that hard of a climb. The trail was already laid out for him. Except for a few places where he had to climb over boulders, the climb was enjoyable and easy. Dante loved walking in nature. The planet was beautiful. The sky was pink and purple like it always was and it gave everything a gentle pink light. The path was littered with wildflowers of all kinds. If he wasn't already on a mission, he would pick a small bouquet for his mother.

When he finally made it to the top of the mountain, there was a single tree where a zilu bird sat, as if she was waiting for his arrival. Dante climbed the tree until he found the nest. Inside the nest, four perfectly green eggs rested. The zilu bird screamed at Dante and puffed out her wings. This startled the young boy and he almost lost his balance but he held on tightly to the tree. He reached for one of the eggs, but before he could even touch it the mother bird swooped down and knocked Dante out of the tree. Dante fell with a thud and had the wind knocked out of him. He lay on the ground for a moment, looking up at the zilu nest. The mother bird sorted through her eggs, counting them to make sure all four of them were there. Dante

The Broken Kingdom of Orion

observed her until one of the moons began to rise over the horizon. He felt saddened for himself, but he watched the mother bird sitting on her nest and realized he didn't want to take her eggs. It would clearly upset her if one of her babies were taken away. Defeated, Dante got up and made his way back down the mountain. He walked through the forest trail, and by the time he made it back to the palace the second moon was high in the sky.

The party inside the palace quickly quieted as the people watched their young prince walk, with his head down in shame, to the king.

"My dear boy, where is the egg you were sent to get," the King asked.

"I didn't get it, father. I failed," Dante said.

"You were unable to get the egg?"

"No, I was able to. I could have gotten it but…" the young boy stopped talking and looked up at his father.

"But what, son?" the King prompted him to continue. Dante tried to ignore the hundreds of eyes that were watching this exchange. He tried to imagine it was just him and his father, but he knew this task was important for the kingdom to have an heir as much as it was for him to succeed. He turned to face the people, his people. He took a breath before announcing to them.

"People of Orion, I'm sorry I failed you. I wanted to succeed and be a good king but… The task meant I had to steal an egg from a mother bird. Her eggs turn into baby birds, and I didn't want to upset her. How would you feel if someone stole your babies? I'm sorry I failed you." Dante lowered his head and the palace erupted in cheers. Dante looked at everyone, confused, as the people began celebrating once again.

Reji Ex

"Well done, my boy. You are going to make a fine king someday." The King hugged his confused son.

"I don't understand. The task was to bring back an egg in perfect condition," Dante said. The King gave a deep, bellowing laugh.

"Yes, that is what you were told, but a true king cannot bring pain or sadness to any of his subjects. That includes the subjects that live in the wild, too. The task is a trick. Anyone can follow orders. It takes a true king to do what is right rather than what is ordered. You have succeeded in your task."

Confetti was thrown, bells rang, cake was eaten, and booze was poured as the whole kingdom cheered and celebrated for their new heir. Dante Lupa was going to be the next King of Orion and the people were overjoyed. They had an heir who would lead them with grace and honor as the kings before.

A few years down the road, Dante was with his father when visitors came. He was supposed to learn the diplomatic part of being king but this was hard for Dante. He wished that he could hire someone else to do it, but his father assured him only the king could. Dante was more interested in keeping the people safe and happy instead of trading with other planet's royalty. The King assured Dante that diplomacy was important for the kingdom's happiness, no matter how boring it was.

"King Luka, Prince Dante, I was wondering if you were interested in a trade deal with the planet Helix," the visiting king asked.

"What is it that you have to offer?" King Luka asked.

"I noticed the planet of Orion lacks military forces. This is very dangerous, my lord. An enemy can attack at any time and you are completely defenseless."

The Broken Kingdom of Orion

King Luka laughed and the servants bustling around the room also stopped to laugh with their king. "Orion is a planet of peace. We have no enemies. No one would senselessly attack our planet. There is no reason to."

"Very well. I can trade you my daughter. I know your young prince is unattached. An arranged marriage would suffice for our trade," the visiting King said. Dante had a flash of fear that perhaps his father would agree to this, but before he even had time to worry, his father waved his hand dismissively.

"Orion doesn't trade people. And it is not our tradition to arrange marriages. We are empathetic people. Having an unhappy queen would hinder our planet greatly," King Luka said. Dante sighed in relief. "My dear friend, it is clear to me that you do not know the ways of Orion. Come join us for a celebration. Learn our customs, and meet our people. Open your mind and hearts to our traditions; that would be enough for a trade. Bring your daughter. We will not force a marriage, but that does not mean they will not fall in love by chance." The visiting king scowled for a moment, then laughed along with the King of Orion.

"Well, that was the simplest trade I have ever made then," he announced. The next day the servants were busy preparing for a royal ball. Dante didn't know it at the time, but his life was soon about to change forever.

Space

Aries stopped talking suddenly and stared out the window of the shuttle. "Then what happened?" Elenora asked.

"I don't like talking about it," he muttered.

Reji Ex

"Why? What happened next?"

"I met my bitch wife."

"My mother?" Elenora asked. Aries looked at her for a moment then quickly looked at his hands resting on his legs. He realized he couldn't keep insulting that woman in front of Elenora. No matter how cruel she was, no matter how much he hated her, that was his baby's mom. Elenora will always be part Nava whether Aries liked it or not.

"Can I tell you a secret?" Aries asked gently, still looking at his hands. "I don't want to be bitter and cynical. I don't like all this—violence and killings. I want my old life back where everyone on the whole planet was happy. If she...if she ever wanted to give up and wanted to come back to me, I'd take her back. Especially since you're alive."

Elenora looked out the window without saying anything in reply. She didn't have a good start on Earth, even before the rest of the kids started showing up. She wasn't too sure if she would ever forgive someone who blew up her home planet, but she figured if someone was raised with nothing but peace and love, who had it suddenly ripped away, they'd want to get it back without too much struggle. She didn't blame him.

13: Eris

Kettle dragged his duffle bag to the basement of the school where the rest of the town was waiting. He made his way to the basement and the crowd hushed when they saw him. They were expecting him to show them something mind blowing that would get them to want to join the revolution. Kettle felt that he was able to deliver on that promise. He got to the center of the room. The town made a circle around him as he dumped the contents of the duffle bag onto the ground.

"What is that?" someone asked.

"That is one of the assistants. I stabbed her this morning," Kettle announced. There were gasps and murmurs in the crowd so he continued. "But it's okay because she was just a robot the entire time. I bet all of them are robots."

"We're being watched by a bunch of robots?" someone shouted.

"We're not even on the queen's radar. She left a bunch of junk to babysit us!"

"What's the plan?" Tovah asked. Kettle looked at her, surprised that she was the

first of the group to ask.

Reji Ex

"Well, first we need to take a vote. Who wants to join the revolution?" Kettle asked. Slowly, everyone raised their hands. The idea that they weren't even being repressed by real people made them change their minds. Others were ready for their old ways of life back. The reason didn't matter, the number of people willing and able to help was what mattered most.

"Alright, then I suggest tomorrow when the robots get to your house, take them out. But be stealthy about it. I don't want anyone to get hurt. Attack them from behind, use something metal to short their circuit," Kettle said. The crowd mumbled their agreement.

"Alright! That was everything for today. Go home, get some sleep. Kettle and I will be here if you have any questions about Earth revolutions," Kayo announced.

Everyone made their way out of the school and back to their homes. Kayo looked over at Kettle, who was waiting with her.

"I guess no one needed to read the book to get on board," she said.

"But you knew they didn't. You wanted to get me alone. Why?" Kettle quesitoned, cutting right to the chase. Kayo fidgeted with her fingers and rocked back and forth on her feet.

"I never really got the chance to thank you for helping me when we got back, for finding my family for me. Everything." Kettle smiled at her.

"It was no big deal," he said.

"It was a big deal. You've seen the condition of this place. Who knows what would have happened to me if you didn't care so much," Kayo said. She stepped closer to him and he began to grow nervous.

"We have to get back to the house," he said.

Kayo gently touched his arm. "I just wanted to thank you," she said. Kettle wasn't a virgin, but he was a gentleman. He only ever slept with women he had been dating at the time. He never got into the one-night-stand hype. Kayo wasn't interested in a relationship at this time. At least, Kettle didn't think she was. The world was too messy and was about to get messier. A relationship was too much of a hassle to start at this point. Maybe after the war they could be together, but right now it was clear to Kettle that Kayo was more interested in letting off some steam.

"Here?" he questioned.

"No one would bother us. We would have privacy," Kayo confirmed.

Kettle wrapped his arms around her waist and kissed her passionately. He lowered her to the ground and began helping her take her clothes off. She pulled off his shirt and continued kissing him.

"If we die tomorrow, I want this to be our last moment together," she whispered to him. He froze for a moment but continued kissing at her neck. He wasn't sure if she had just confessed feelings for him or if she was just stating she wanted lovemaking to be her last act before dying in a war. Kettle did not like one-night-stands, and he did not like casual sex with friends. He was a feelings person, and if the sex was meant to be meaningless then he was left confused. He pushed his confusing thoughts aside as he entered Kayo. He moved in her and kissed at her neck, nipping her ear lobe until he felt her pleasure. When he was sure she had her fulfillment, he finished in her. Kettle rolled off of her and laid beside her, pulling her into his arms.

"Tomorrow, if everyone kills one robot, it'll make a dent and the queen might notice and attack us," Kayo said.

"Let's not worry about that right now. We can worry about it tomorrow. We should get dressed and get back," Kettle said. Kayo didn't move.

"I just want a few more minutes. Do you think we can be together when this is over?" she asked. Kettle blinked. She did have feelings for him.

"It's possible," he said, kissing her lips. She cuddled into him more. They lay silently for a while, eventually getting dressed and leaving without another word. When they got home, they got into their beds and went to sleep as if nothing happened between them.

The next day, the two families were ready for the knock at the door. Kojo opened the door and the assistant walked in with their telltale smile and signature line about serving the queen. Then Kojo stabbed her in the back with a knife. The bot jolted as electric currents sparked from its body before falling to the ground.

"Okay? Now what? Do we go to work now? Do we…just hang out?" Tovah asked.

"I think we should work. At least the animals need to be cared for," Argo said. The families went to work at their respective jobs. They worked all day, and at the end of the workday, another assistant showed up.

Argo wasn't sure if it was the repetitiveness of every day being the same as the last, or maybe the talk of revolution, or just plain exhaustion from working, but something inside her snapped when she heard the same thing she'd heard every day for the past five years. She whipped the hot tray around and bashed the bot in the face. The bot stumbled back, face half-melted off from the heat.

"The queen would not be pleased—" she started, but Argo cut her off with another hit to the face and another and another, causing the bot to fall to the ground. She continued to bash the robot's head in until it stopped moving. The robot gave a couple of weak gear-clicking noises before shutting down.

"Are you alright?" Tovah asked. Before Argo could reply, a few more bots came into the bakery with guns. Argo and Tovah ducked behind the counter as the bots opened fire. They flattened themselves against the ground until the gunfire ceased.

They didn't dare move until they heard the bots leave.

Kettle and Kojo ran through the door. "Mom?" Kettle called out.

"I'm alright. Tovah?" Argo said.

"I'm fine. What was that?" Tovah asked.

"I don't know…wait…" Argo said. She walked around the counter and noticed that the bot was gone. The others took it. "I think I know what happened. I think when the bot saw me trying to kill it, it sent out a signal."

"You killed a bot?"

"Yes. Well, I saw you do it once," Argo said in defense.

"But the bot was looking at her when she did it. And it wasn't quick either," Tovah said.

"Okay, we definitely need to let the town know this so no one gets hurt," Kojo said. Elma and Kayo were already in the house when the rest of the family went in.

"I don't think Tovah and Argo should be seen by any bots anymore," Kojo said.

"I was thinking the same thing. If they saw you and tried to gun you down then saw you again they might try again," Kettle said. Kettle caught Kayo and Elma up on what happened in the bakery.

"Food rations will get low if they aren't counted," Elma said.

Reji Ex

"We can make it work. I just don't know who will run the bakery," Argo said.

"Are you hearing yourself? They tried to kill you and you're more worried about serving them," Elma snapped at her sister.

"Let's take this conversation to the basement?" Kayo suggested. Argo's eyes widened with fear. Kojo peeked out the window and signaled for the families to go downstairs. There was a knock at the door and Kojo hesitantly opened it.

"Yes?" he asked.

"We have received noise complaints from this house," the bot said. This was a ridiculous phrase that they often said when they overheard a conversation. They had no neighbors to complain about noise for the bots to use this as an excuse.

"I am very sorry. My wife...she died unexpectedly today. My son and I were just grieving," Kojo said.

"Refrain from grieving so loud in the future," the bot said. Kojo barely had time to close the door before bullets started flying through the walls and in the windows. He dropped to the floor and crawled to the basement door. He safely made it into the basement and got the families to cover.

"They can't go underground. We're safe down here," Kojo said.

"We're not safe on this planet," Kettle replied. The gunfire stopped and it was assumed that the robots had left.

"Is this because we started a revolution?" Tovah asked.

"No, because they don't know it was us. This was because they overheard our defiant conversation. They heard that you and Argo survived," Elma said.

"So we're trapped down here? If we go up then they'll hear us and kill us?" Kayo said, beginning to panic.

The Broken Kingdom of Orion

"No, we get to the town meeting and tell them what happened. They'll help us. They have to," Argo said.

"They don't have to. They can see this as a reason to go back to how things were and abandon us," Tovah said.

"Why don't we just ask them directly? Tonight. We get there quietly. Pack your bags," Kojo instructed.

In the cover of night, the families made their way to the school for what would be their last time. Kettle looked at his old childhood home. If all went well with the revolution then he would be returning, but nothing was promised after today. The family's safety came first. That was the only thing he knew for certain. They got to the school as everyone else was gathering for the town meeting.

"First of all, is everyone alright?" Kojo asked.

"We were shot at!"

"We were too. This isn't safe for us," someone shouted.

"Did anyone get killed?" Kojo asked. No one answered. "Alright so everyone is safe. We've concluded that if the bots see you killing them, they have a kill safe to contact more bots to take you out. This is an anti-revolution tactic, we assume."

"So, what is the plan now?"

"You still want to go through with this?" Tovah questioned.

"Yes! The queen can't send robots to stalk us. To make sure we worship her and live our lives the way she wants us to. We're sick of it!" someone yelled. The crowd cheered in agreement.

"We can't survive living in this basement without food," Tovah said.

"We can all move here," someone suggested.

"We can avoid our jobs and go out and loot the bots for food," someone else said.

Reji Ex

"You want to provoke the queen and the robots?"

"Yes! Start a revolution!" someone shouted.

"Revolution!" the crowd began to chant. "Revolution! Revolution!"

"I guess we really made a difference," Kayo whispered to Kettle. He nodded and slipped his hand into hers.

"We can really save our planet."

14: Battleship Juniper

Elenora and her friends followed Aries as they entered the massive ship. The ship was still decorated lavishly as if it were still being used as a cruise ship. Only a few changes here and there. Crewmen saluted Aries as he walked by and one even got him a cigar and lit it for him.

"You know smoking is really bad for you?" Elenora said. Aries glared at her for a moment then softened his gaze, as if he had needed a second to remember that she was his daughter.

"That is something I will work on for you," he said begrudgingly. Elenora smiled at his attempt to be a good dad for her. Aries led the group through a door where Marko, Roman, and Besnik were waiting for them. Elenora squealed with delight and ran up to hug Marko. Marko held her protectively and glared at Aries.

"Why did you bring us here?" Marko demanded.

"Marko," Roman scolded under his breath. Aries gave Marko a smirk.

"You mean why did I bring my daughter here? Well, because she's my daughter," Aries said. Marko gasped. "Oh, didn't you

Reji Ex

know? Your little princess is...well...a princess. Princess Elenora Lupa of Orion to be exact."

"Did you know this?" Marko asked Elenora.

"I actually found out today!" Elenora said with a smile. Marko looked between her and Aries.

"And Vine and Jax?"

"Well, we wanted to come to fight the war with you," Vine said.

"War that he started," Marko said.

"Hmm, can confirm that he did not start the war. I actually blew up a planet in the name of the queen," Roman said.

"It was my planet, Helix," Besnik said. Marko stopped talking.

"Look, Marko, there isn't a person on this ship who wouldn't go to battle to protect Aries and his crew, so maybe just relax with the allegations. Besides, he's your father-in-law now," Roman told his brother.

"Why don't you take Elenora to see your room? If you need anything, don't hesitate to ask my crew. Oh, and Kuiporian? Don't touch my daughter," Aries said. Roman cracked up laughing but Marko turned red and led Elenora away. Jax and Vine followed them.

Marko led the group to a room that was a lot larger than the other rooms. It had an added-on room that was clearly once a lavish rec center with a gaming table, video game devices, a mini fridge, and a seating area. Next to the king-sized bed was a large window with long drapes that caressed the sides of it. It was the king's suite that was revamped for a group of young adults to hang out in. Aries was clearly the one who redid the room so Elenora and her friends had a place to hang out.

"This is your room?" Vine asked Marko.

The Broken Kingdom of Orion

"Well, I was upgraded when the king heard that the princess was married to me," Marko said.

"Are you…mad at me about this?" Elenora asked.

"Of course, I'm not mad. I just feel like I don't know you as well as I thought I did," he said.

"Marko! I was left on Earth as a baby. I didn't know this either," Elenora protested.

Marko sighed in defeat. "You're right. I'm sorry. This was just a surprise is all,"

"Oh yeah and I totally expected this," Elenora said sarcastically.

"Okay, what are we going to do about this? About any of this?" Jax asked the group.

"Well, I guess we'll just help out where we can," Vine said, plopping herself down on one of the sofas. Jax sat across from her.

"No, I mean…Isn't he the deranged king? The one that went crazy and like, genocided his whole planet? The one from the story." Marko blinked at Jax in confusion.

"That doesn't sound right. When I was a kid, we were told stories about a magical land that was ruled by a gracious king," Marko said. Jax shrugged.

"Maybe the story changes from planet to planet. You're from Kuiper, right? I'm from Helix," Jax said. Elenora looked at him with concern.

"Wait, the planet that Roman blew up?" Elenora said. Jax scoffed and rolled his eyes.

"No one can blow up a planet," Jax said.

"Well, yeah. Orion is taught on Earth as being a nebula. Helix too. The planet is gone," Marko said. Jax rolled his eyes again at the comment.

Reji Ex

"Jax? What's going on?" Vine said. Jax looked at his friends who were looking at him with concern and fear. He chuckled as if he was joking.

"Guys, nothing is wrong. It was just a story. Like the Cat in the Hat," he said. The friends looked at each other, not really buying that excuse.

"We're all friends here, man. Just tell us what's going on," Marko said. Jax looked out the window, then back to his friends.

"I told you. This was just the story from my planet. The King of Orion is evil. He kidnapped a princess from Helix and held her captive for years. That's the story. That's it."

"You think Aries is this king?" Elenora asked. Jax shrugged.

"He is the only one that survived from Orion. Doesn't that seem weird? Like there's literally just him and Elenora left from this evil planet," Jax said.

"Why did you volunteer to come if that's how you felt about him?" Vine asked.

"Isn't it obvious? To get evidence that he's evil and end the war. Like I said, I want to help end the war and go home," Jax said.

"Home, as in Nevada?" Vine asked. Jax chuckled.

"Vine, I'm not going back to Earth. I mean Helix."

"Helix is gone, though," Elenora said.

"Wait, you told me that you and I were gonna be together!" Vine snapped.

"Well, honey, I assumed after the war you would want to go back to Makemake. Just like how I would want to go back to Helix," Jax said.

Vine stood up abruptly. "So you were just using me this whole time?!" she screamed.

The Broken Kingdom of Orion

"No, we were having fun," Jax responded. Vine stormed out of the room and slammed the door shut. With tears freely flowing down her face, she walked through the massive halls of the ship. She quickly realized that she didn't know where she was going. The reality of being on a ship away from anything familiar was starting to weigh on her. She sat down in the hallways and pulled her knees up to her chest and buried her face. She heard people passing her without bothering her. Then she heard someone say "Yeah that's her." and "Okay, I'll take care of it." She felt a gentle tap on her shoulder and looked up to see Aries.

"You want some ice cream?" he offered. She wiped her tears and nodded. Aries helped her up and guided her to the kitchen. She sat down at a table and Aries gathered anything she might need to make a giant ice cream sundae.

"I might not be the best with women but I do know when you see one crying you offer ice cream," Aries said. Vine started digging into the ice cream straight out of the container.

"I just…I thought we were gonna be together. I thought he was the one. You know?" Vine vented. Aries nodded.

"I get it. My ex-wife was the love of my life. And now she's-"

"A backstabbing lying jerk that was just using me for a good time. Didn't even want a future with me on Earth!"

"Yeah…"

"I never wanted to go back to Makemake. I wanted to stay on Earth. I loved Earth. It's beautiful, and I felt like I belonged there. Makemake is cold and rainy. And they're weird about women being babymakers. I hate babies. And Jax said he wanted to be with me and now I learn that he wants to go back to Helix," Vine ranted.

"What changed?" Aries asked. Vine filled her mouth with whipped cream.

"He met you and believes you're some evil kidnapper or whatever. I really wasn't paying attention to his reason at all," Vine said.

"Guys are jerks," Aries said, just agreeing with the sad woman.

"They are the worst! Except you. And Marko. Ugh, Marko's love for Elenora was why I thought dating Jax would be fine. Marko said he would come back for her when they didn't know if she was ever gonna leave Earth. Now look where we are! On the spaceship that Marko summoned to get back to his wife!" Vine snapped.

"Yup," Aries said for lack of words. He was happy to hear that Marko was truly in love with his daughter and that it made other women jealous, but his current mission was to make Vine feel better. Perhaps ranting was her way to blow off steam, but Aries knew that food was the best way to calm people down. Vine sniffled in her ice cream.

"Elenora is my best friend. I'm happy that she has someone like Marko. I just…I want to go back to Earth. I was promised an Earth life," Vine said. Aries thought for a moment.

"Okay, I have to pick up the kids from Eris. Then I can drop you off at Earth with the rest of them. But I can't take you back just yet. How can I make you feel better right now?" Aries asked. Vine fluttered her eyelashes.

"I want to learn a skill that can help me on Earth. I want to be prepared to live my life as a single woman in America," Vine said. Aries nodded.

"Okay! I can help you with that," he said.

"Really?" Vine smiled.

The Broken Kingdom of Orion

"Yeah, we can go right now, actually. What do you want to learn?"

"IT. I can get a job anywhere and make a lot of money with IT. I started learning it on Earth," Vine said.

"Sounds like you've been thinking about this for a while," Aries said. He stood up and Vine followed him.

"I always wanted to go into the field but I thought Jax and I would be together."

"Word of advice, never sacrifice yourself for someone else. Even if you love them. If they love you then you won't have to change who you are."

"You're right," Vine said. Aries led her to a room full of computers with workers at every station. When they saw Aries enter, they all stood and saluted.

"This is Vine. I want you to teach her everything you know. I want her to be the best IT personnel on this ship when we take her back to Earth," Aries ordered. The crew responded, "Yes captain!" and Vine was taken away by the computer crew willing to teach her. "Oh, and Vine! Just so you know, your room is the one directly next to Elenora's. The crew will show you when you're ready."

Aries walked out of the room as Vine was being taught the basics of IT.

After Vine left, Jax followed suit and left the couple alone in their room. "Is that what you think, too?" Elenora asked softly.

Reji Ex

"What? What Jax said? No, I just...Roman told me that he's killed people for following the queen. That's not okay," Marko said.

"Yeah, but Roman said he blew up a planet for the queen too. So maybe the queen's forces are the bad guys here and need to be killed," Elenora said.

"You don't really think that. No one deserves death," Marko said.

"At least we know for a fact that there were innocent people on the planet your brother blew up."

Marko sighed in frustration. He knew there was no use arguing with her. Really, there wasn't an argument. Both sides have done bad things, and it was clear that Elenora was going to defend her new father.

"We've had a long day. Why don't we go to sleep and when we are more rested, we can talk more," Marko said.

"There's nothing to talk about. I'm siding with Aries," Elenora said.

"I understand that. You feel like you have to because he's your father, but you just met this man. He might be...he might—"

"Oh what? Be the deranged king in Jax's fairytale?"

"Elenora, Jax is right about one thing. You two are the only ones that survived. That can't be a coincidence," Marko said.

"You're right. It was planned. I was kidnapped by someone who knew about the explosion and Aries followed to find me," Elenora explained. Marko was taken aback and relaxed his anger at Aries for a second.

"Did he tell you that?"

"Yes! And he said it was my mother that blew up the planet in the first place," Elenora said. Marko scratched his head. Elenora continued, "Yeah. You don't know what you're talking about either."

The Broken Kingdom of Orion

Elenora and Marko were silent for the rest of the night. The next morning, Elenora silently woke up and made her way to the cafeteria for breakfast. She went to sit at a table but was stopped by a crewman.

"Actually, Captain wanted you to see him. He's in the kitchen," they said.

Elenora felt nervous as she walked to the kitchen. She wasn't quite sure what to expect. She knew Jax was probably wrong about him being deranged, but she also knew Marko was right about her not knowing Aries at all. When she walked through the kitchen, one of the cooks pointed to a room in the back. She pushed through the door. Aries and a couple of other people were sitting around a table. Aries saw Elenora enter and waved her over to the table.

"Oh, look who it is! Proof that Aries does have d-" Roman started.

"How was your night, Princess," Besnik said, cutting off Roman.

"Princess? Oh right…my night was okay," Elenora said.

"Your friend made it sound like there was some trouble," Aries said.

"What did she say to you?" Elenora said, concerned that Vine told him what Jax was saying last night. Aries just shrugged.

"Boys are stupid and she was planning on going back to Earth someday," Aries said. Elenora sighed in relief. "Oh, were you expecting her to tell me that your friends are divided on whether I'm evil or not?"

Elenora stiffened, and her eyes widened. Roman laughed at her reaction. Aries gestured to an empty chair at the table.

"Sit. Let's talk. Get to know each other. I don't want you to be on the fence about me," he said. Elenora cautiously sat in the chair that was set for her.

"You didn't care that I thought you were a bad guy," Roman said.

"I still don't. Okay, Elenora, ask anything you want. Nothing's off limits," Aries said.

"Can I ask a question?" Roman asked.

"No."

"Well, Jax brought up a good point. Why were you the only one that survived the explosion?" Elenora asked. Aries frowned and looked away.

"Okay. The answer to that doesn't really help in interrogations. I have no idea how I survived. I just remember running to get my baby, you. And you were gone and then I woke up later. Off the planet and alone," Aries explained.

"Why do you have Marko's brother on your ship?" Elenora asked.

"I kidnapped him. Kidnapped everyone on the ship really. They stay because they want to. I give them the choice to leave."

"Or die?" Elenora asked.

"Look, killing isn't something I like doing. And it's not something I do often. But this is a war, and some people aren't able to be saved from…her," Aries said.

"The bloodthirsty murder queen that kidnaps children," Roman said.

"The mother of my child, who is sitting in front of us," Aries said to Roman.

"Why is she kidnapping the children?" Elenora questioned.

"No clue, but we are going to find out," Aries said.

"I have a theory. When she came to Kuiper, they killed my parents and took my brother. The queen's men told me that if I joined her then the war would be over sooner and I could have my brother back," Roman said.

"So, she's manipulating families with their kids," Elenora concluded.

"I think so. Why multiple planets, I don't know. What outcome she's going for? I don't know. I do know we're going to put a stop to it," Roman said. Elenora began to relax when she realized Aries's goal was to stop someone from kidnapping children to manipulate planets of people. That was a good guy motive.

"And it's my mother that's doing all this. Will… will I become evil too?" Elenora asked.

Aries looked at her.

"Have you ever felt someone else's pain? Like, not 'put yourself in their shoes' but actually felt it?" he asked. Elenora thought for a moment.

"I think so. Why?" she asked.

"What about the people around you? Do they seem happier when you're happy or do they argue with you and each other when you're in a bad mood?" Aries asked.

"Well, yes. Last night my husband was arguing with me. I thought we just weren't seeing eye to eye, but the argument kept going in circles," Elenora said.

"Hmm…interesting," Aries said.

"Why?"

"Orions are special. They are empaths, and they don't harm anyone because the emotions that harming people causes…well, it makes us sad," Aries explained.

"Sooo…you don't think I'm capable of hurting people?" Elenora asked. Aries looked at his daughter and smiled gently.

Reji Ex

"I don't think you are capable of causing pain," he said. The cook brought in plates of food for the four sitting at the table. Elenora looked at it. The plate consisted of eggs, toast, pancakes, and sausage.

"Earth food?" she asked.

"For you, Princess," the cook said. She smiled at the cook.

"Thank you," she said before digging into the eggs.

"Aries is treated like a beloved king here. Thought it was weird and cult-like until I learned that he actually was a beloved king," Roman said.

"Aries is special. He just…has a vibe around him. Like you know he's genuine," Besnik said. Elenora kept eating.

"You know, my father always said that food tricks the mind into thinking it's safe. In nature, animals only eat when they are safe. Of course, whenever my father was around you were safe but he would feed his guests to make them safe," Aries said.

"That's why you called me to have breakfast with you? To trick me into feeling safe with you?" Elenora asked.

"Trick you? You're too smart for that. Telling you the truth, no tricks needed. Plus, you're a Lupa, so you can tell when people are lying anyways," Aries said.

"Prove it," Elenora demanded.

"Okay, let me think. Umm.. when I was five I had a pet zilu bird named Rex. My mother was a commoner from Orion. The best day of my life was the birth of my daughter," Aries said. He leaned forward, waiting for Elenora to answer.

"Zilu bird one was the lie," she said. Aries gave a proud smirk and leaned back in his seat.

"Orion, through and through. Owning a zilu bird and taking it from the wild was a crime on my planet. Although some zilu birds would land on people's shoulders. It was the royal symbol of the Lupa family," Aries said.

"Lupa. My last name?"

"Yes. I thought you knew that. You had your bracelet the whole time, right?" Aries asked.

"Yeah but…it's just blinking lights isn't it?"

Aries laughed. "It was turned off so I thought you knew how to use it. Well, it's nothing special. It just tells you about the family history. Press any of the buttons. It's holographic and interactable," Aries said. Elenora pressed on one of the blinking lights and a tree lit up above the bracelet. The tree had names written on it. It was a family tree. She held her hand up to the holograph and made a motion to zoom in. It worked like an Earth cell phone. She found her name at the roots of the tree and a little further up she found Nava Nui of Helix and Dante Lupa of Orion.

"Dante? I thought your name was Aries," she said. Aries looked away.

"Dante was someone else. I'm not him anymore."

Elenora felt as if she understood what Aries meant. Given what he had told her about Orion, she figured that what Aries had done in the name of winning a war was enough to make him feel as if he didn't deserve his Orion name. Elenora pushed the next button. A holographic picture of Aries holding a baby came to view. He looked up and smiled.

"Are you recording this?" the video image asked.

"Yes. I am. I was gonna make a video diary for her to look back on," a woman's voice said from behind the camera. The video Aries laughed.

"If you say so."

"Tell her something you want her to know," the woman said. Aries looked down at the baby in his arms. "No, no. I mean look at the camera and say it so she has something to look back on."

Aries smiled and looked at the camera. "This feels silly."

"You'll be happy you have this one day."

"Okay. Hi Elenora. I'm your dad. I don't know what to say. Umm…you're going to replace me someday and I can't wait to see you become an amazing queen. I'm gonna be with you every step of the way," the man in the video stopped to smile at the baby in his arms. "Daddy loves you more than anything, Elenora."

Aries reached over the table and snatched the bracelet away from Elenora. He pushed his chair back causing it to fall over and went over to the window. He stared out for a moment. No one in the room knew what to do.

"That was one of the last times I saw my daughter," Aries said after a moment of silence. He laughed to himself and turned around. "I'm sorry. My daughter is a touchy subject to me. I almost forgot."

Aries handed the bracelet back to Elenora.

Marko entered the room. "There you are," he said. He glanced at Aries but sat next to Elenora.

"Aries was just telling me about my family history," Elenora said.

"Why's Roman here?" Marko asked.

"He won't leave me alone, no matter how many times I threaten him," Aries answered, going back to his own chair and putting it upright.

"You'd never hurt me. You love me," Roman teased.

"I've literally killed someone for saying that to me before," Aries said.

The Broken Kingdom of Orion

"The real question is, why is Besnik here," Roman said.

"He's too much of a coward to be left alone. Plus, I trust him," Aries answered.

Aries continued eating his breakfast. "So, Marko, don't you think it's a little rude to date someone's daughter when you're planning their assassination?"

"Woah, I wasn't planning any assassination!" Marko said, defending himself.

"Yeah, Marko. That's pretty Hamlet of you. I thought I raised you better," Roman teased.

"What?" Marko questioned.

"You know, stabbing your father-in-law through a curtain,"

"I understood what you meant. I just don't know how you know about an Earth writer," Marko said. Roman looked at Marko with confusion.

"Shakespear isn't from Earth," he said.

"If I remember correctly, Hamlet died after killing his father-in-law," Aries said with a smirk. Marko sat back in his chair.

"Oh, I see. You're terrorizing me," Marko said.

"And you're having sex with my daughter."

"Aries!" Elenora yelled. She buried her face in her hands in embarrassment.

Marko stared at Aries who just stared back.

"Gee Marko, didn't you know you can't taint royal blood like that?" Roman said.

Without looking, Aries undid his sidearm and aimed it at Roman.

"What are you doing?!" Marko shrieked. Roman just smirked.

"Oh please, do it," Roman said. Aries shook his head. He put his gun back in his holster with a chuckle.

Reji Ex

"What is going on here?" Marko demanded. Roman looked at his confused brother and laughed.

"This is what guys do, Marko," Besnik said.

"Marko was always a little sensitive, like Besnik," Roman said.

"I was not!" Marko protested.

"Am I supposed to be offended?" Besnik asked.

"Aries is unhinged. He's killed people," Marko said.

"This again?" Aries said.

"You were just about to shoot my brother!"

"With this?" Aries pulled out his gun and shot Marko in the forehead with a dart.

"Ow! What the fuck?"

"I have to shoot Roman like ten times a day. He doesn't leave me alone," Aries explained. Aries set his gun on the table and slid it over to Marko. "Go ahead. Try it."

"Marko, don't," Elenora whispered to him. Marko picked up the gun and studied it for a moment. It looked like a real gun but its weight was lighter, as if it was made of plastic. Aries watched him, smirking.

"Marko doesn't believe in violence. He had one mishap but he'd never do anything violent ever again," Roman said. Marko aimed the gun at Aries and shot at him. The dart hit Aries in the chest with a thunk.

"Ouch."

"Oh, I guess he does choose violence now," Roman said. Marko emptied the whole chamber at Aries. When there were no more darts left in the gun, he set it back on the table and slid it over.

"Do you feel better? Get some of that anger towards me out?" Aries asked.

The Broken Kingdom of Orion

Elenora stood up and walked out of the room. Marko quickly followed her.

"I'm sorry," he said.

"For what? Shooting my father or for calling him unhinged when you were the one that emptied a gun on him," Elenora said.

"It was a toy gun. He's not actually shot." Elenora stopped and looked at him.

"Do you trust me, Marko?" she asked.

"Of course, I do. You're my wife."

"Okay well, I trust Aries. And I think he's a good guy. And that he's being upfront and honest with us. His methods are…off, but overall, I trust him," she said. Marko looked like he was about to protest or fight back in some way but he sighed and nodded.

"Alright, I trust your judgment. I will attempt to be less of a jerk to Aries. And just so you know I'm serious, I will try to convince Jax that Aries is not as bad of a guy as he thinks," Marko begrudgingly said. Elenora smiled at her husband. They started to walk back to their room when they passed a group standing idly on the side of the room.

"That's the princess, let's drop everything and worship her," someone said mockingly. Elenora whipped around.

"Excuse me?" she demanded. She was face to face with a girl that was nearly double her size with muscles to match. She had a stereotypical "tough girl" looking tattoo on her face. She was a walking bully cliche with the attitude.

"Oh, I'm sorry. Did I forget to curtsy for you?" the girl said. Her friends tried to tell her to stop, that the captain wouldn't be too happy about this, but the girl shrugged them off. Elenora held her head up.

Reji Ex

"Actually, you did. Bow before me," Elenora said. Marko leaned against the wall and crossed his arms. Elenora was normally a timid girl, but in recent years The General taught her how to fight to defend herself against bullies.

"This is going to be fun," he muttered to himself.

The girl laughed. "Oh, are you gonna make me?" she said, pushing Elenora's shoulder.

"I don't need to make you. I'm the princess, the captain's daughter. You're going to," Elenora demanded. The girl swung at Elenora which she easily blocked and redirected. Elenora had the girl's arm pinned behind her back. "My god, do you have any technique? You can't just make muscle tone and call it good. Here, try again."

Elenora kicked the girl back to her side. A crowd was forming around the two girls. The girl roared and charged at Elenora. Elenora used the girl's shoulders to jump right over her.

"You know, on Earth, there's a sport where people do that but they use dumb bulls instead of dumb bitches," Elenora said. The crowd began to cheer and jeer. They took sides and bets. Elenora was small but she was definitely more skilled and agile than the other girl. Not only that, but she was the captain's daughter and people were nervous to bet against her. Others voted for the mean girl that they'd known for a while, the bigger girl with bigger muscles that they'd seen in a fight before.

"Why don't you try one more time before I get a hit in," Elenora said. The girl laughed.

"You'll never get a hit on me," she said. She took another swing at Elenora who used the momentum of the punch against the girl and pinned her to the ground. Elenora took a handful of the girl's hair and smashed her head into the ground, knocking her out. The crowd cheered. The girl stumbled to get up, her face was bloody from just the one hit. She drunkenly tried to swing at Elenora again, but Elenora grabbed her fist to stop it.

"Oh my god, you seriously only have punching in your tool belt. This is sad. Especially when I can do this," Elenora twisted the girl's arm into a position where she could break it at the elbow. The girl screamed in pain.

"What is going on here?!" Elenora heard Aries yell. She slowly turned to see him pushing his way through the crowd. He stopped when he saw his daughter and a woman twice her size writhing in pain on the ground beside her.

"I...I can explain," Elenora whispered. Aries held up his hand and Elenora stopped talking. She looked down. Aries turned to the crowd that was watching with bated breath.

"So, let me guess. Selma decided to challenge the new person and met her match?" Aries asked the crowd. A few people nodded silently answering. "Well? Does anyone else want to challenge my daughter?"

No one moved. Aries pulled Elenora in front of him.

"Really? No one at all? That's strange. Selma can't be the only brave one to go head-to-head with MY daughter," Aries said. No one answered. The crowd was so silent that you could hear a pin drop. Aries pointed out two men from the crowd. "You two. Take that idiot to Doc. And after he's treated her wounds, get her off my ship." Aries led Elenora away and glared at Marko as he passed him.

"Great job defending your wife," he muttered to Marko. Marko could help but laugh.

145

Reji Ex

"Did you see the bloody mess that girl left in? And her arm broke in half? Dude, Elenora gave two hits. She does not need to be defended," Marko said. In the hallway, Aries stopped to look at Marko. "No, stop and think about what you're going to say. I've known Elenora for years. Elenora was trained in any fighting style that The General wanted her to know for her own safety. I knew this. I also saw that the girl's friends actively protested her actions. It was going to be a one-on-one fight."

"You should have done something," Aries said.

"I stayed out of El's way," Marko said. Aries shook his head.

"I think Aries is worried about my safety regardless of my fighting skills. Aries has a traumatic response when his daughter, who was stolen from him, is in danger. Doesn't matter if she's actually in danger or not," Elenora said.

"Is that true?" Marko asked.

"I don't know about all that, but…" Aries said. "Yesterday, I only had one goal and it was to take out Nava for what she did to me. Now I have to save another planet, and I also have to take care of Elenora."

"I can actually take care of myself," Elenora said.

Aries shook his head. "I have to fix our broken relationship."

"Our relationship isn't broken. I just…didn't grow up with you as my dad. That's not broken, just paused," Elenora said. Aries chuckled.

"Your husband thinks I'm a homicidal maniac and your friend thinks I blew up my own planet," Aries said.

"I can think that and respect you as a person," Marko said. Aries looked at Marko.

"Just protect her, whether she needs it or not. Can you do that for me?" Aries asked.

The Broken Kingdom of Orion

"Is Elenora's safety the only thing you care for?" Marko asked.

"Absolutely." Aries walked away. Aries went from being a king of a highly emotional feeling planet to feeling as if he needed to protect himself and his emotions. He was unable to talk about his thoughts and unable to adequately process his feelings. Truthfully, yes, he was overly sensitive about Elenora's safety. Losing her left a deep scar in his life that he didn't know he wanted to fix until he got her back. He wasn't an emotionless war machine.

He wanted to change. To be the person he used to be before he was so deeply hurt.

15: Battleship Juniper

A few days later, Vine sat on her bed while Jax sat across from her in a chair.

"I didn't mean to upset you. I thought we were on the same page," Jax said.

"You told me that you wanted an Earth life. I want a life on Earth. If you don't that's fine, but we can't be together anymore if this is going nowhere," Vine said.

"I heard you got a new job on the ship. That's exciting," Jax said. Vine looked at him. He came to her to try to talk things out but quickly changed the subject.

"Yeah, I did. Why?"

"I just think that's so cool! Like, you were always the homemaker type. The perfect housewife. And now you're a working girl. It's cute." Vine stared at him for a moment.

"Cute?" she questioned. Jax shrugged.

"Yeah, like pretend," he said. Vine squinted at him.

"Were you always a sexist asshole? Or did the space air affect your brain?" she asked. Jax laughed.

The Broken Kingdom of Orion

"I'm sorry. You're right. I do sound sexist. Hey, housewife, go to the kitchen and make me a sandwich," Jax joked. Vine didn't laugh, though. Jax sobered up and looked at her. "I'm sorry for being such a jerk. I do care about you."

"You told me you wanted an Earth life with me," Vine stated. Jax nodded.

"I did. I did say that. I wanted it for a while too. Especially when I thought going home wasn't an option. I wanted a life with you, but we're from two different planets," Jax explained.

"I'm going back to Earth. Aries told me he'd take me," Vine said. Jax shook his head and looked down at the floor.

"Please, please don't trust him. He's a bad guy," Jax whispered.

"Why do you keep saying that? You don't even know him."

"Because…It's complicated. The woman that he's hunting, Queen Nava, was the one that took me to Earth. Directly," Jax said.

"What do you mean?"

"She told me about what happened on Orion. How she barely escaped from Aries. She had her daughter hidden on Earth."

"Elenora? You know what happened to Elenora when she got to Earth. If the Queen knew that was happening to her, why didn't she come back for her?"

"She sent me to protect her from that and to make sure Aries didn't find her," Jax said.

"So, you failed your secret mission?"

"Well, yeah. But I came to try to…get rid of him," Jax said slowly.

"Like…kill him?"

"Or get him to turn himself in. Or just capture him myself."

Reji Ex

"So, this, us, Earth, the trip to rescue Eris, was all a trick?" Vine asked.

"Eris doesn't need to be rescued. It's under the queen's control. But Aries, he needs to be taken out. And I'm gonna do it and save the galaxy," Jax said.

"You're here because you want something from me? Not because you wanted to talk out our relationship," Vine concluded.

"I need access to the navigation to get Aries to fly the ship to Ceres. The queen has a prison there. Aries would be stopped, Elenora would be reunited with her mother, I'd be a hero," Jax said. Vine shook her head. "Please, Vine. The fate of the galaxy is relying on you."

"I'm not going to hurt Aries. He's a good man," Vine said.

"No! No, Vine. He's not. Can you just stop being so stupid for a second and see the truth?" Jax snapped. He stood up and towered over her. "You're in with the IT crowd now. I need to redirect the ship to Ceres."

Vine stood up and pushed Jax away from her.

"Get out of my room," Vine yelled at him. Jax roughly grabbed her arm and pinned her to the bed. "Get off me!"

"I don't want to hurt you, but I will if you give me no choice," he whispered to her.

Vine screamed as loud as she could. Jax put his hand over her mouth to silence her. "Vine, I just need-"

Jax was cut off by the door being kicked in.

"Jax, what are you doing?" Marko yelled as he entered the room. He pulled Jax off of Vine and punched him in the face. Elenora went over to Vine and helped her up.

"This isn't what it looks like," Jax said.

The Broken Kingdom of Orion

"No, he was threatening me to get me to–"

Jax cut Vine off abruptly. "She doesn't know what she's talking about.".

"Jax, shut up. Vine, what happened?" Marko asked.

"He wants to reroute the ship to Ceres."

"What?" Roman said from the doorway. Roman walked into the room. "You can't take us to Ceres. That's a prison planet. Everyone here would be executed for treason."

"It's not like that. I...I don't think Vine understood what I meant," Jax said.

"No but we understand that you had her pinned to the bed and you were trying to silence her. We saw that part," Marko said.

"What? Jax, what the hell?" Roman looked at Jax in horror.

"She wouldn't stop screaming and she wouldn't listen to me," Jax defended.

"She doesn't owe you an audience. If she didn't want to listen to you in her own room then you had to leave," Elenora said. Jax shrugged Marko off of him.

"Alright, I'm leaving. This was just a misunderstanding. Sorry," Jax said. He started to walk away but Roman followed him.

"Umm...no. You're gonna come with me," he said.

"I didn't do anything wrong."

"You assaulted a woman to help you commit treason. You're coming with me," Roman said. Jax took off running out of the room and down the hall.

"See, running just makes you look more guilty." Roman got his phone out and called Aries.

"I just saw you five minutes ago, you clingy-" Aries started but Roman cut him off. "That friend of Elenora's, I think his name is Jax, he needs to be captured right now. Do not trust him. He's trying to steer us to Ceres and assaulted that girl you talked to the other night," he told Aries. Aries disconnected the call and a ding on the intercom went off.

"Attention crew, please apprehend the Helixian, Jax. He is wanted for treason and assault. Thank you," the intercom said.

"Vine, are you alright?" Roman asked. Vine nodded. "Well, I was coming over to see if Marko wanted to hit the game room, but now I would prefer if we stayed together for Vine's safety until Jax is caught."

"Yeah. Our room has a gaming system. We can all hang out next door," Marko suggested. The group walked over to Elenora and Marko's room and locked the door behind them. The boys played video games and Vine and Elenora watched from the sitting area. After a few minutes, there was a knock at the door. Elenora went to answer it and looked through the peephole.

"It's Aries," she announced before opening the door. When Aries entered, Vine ran to him and hugged him. Elenora felt a ping of jealousy that Vine seemed to have a better father-daughter relationship with him than her.

"Are you alright?" he asked her. Vine burst into tears.

"I'm fine but it was so scary. He came over to my room and said he wanted to talk about our relationship, but he got so aggressive when I said I wouldn't help him hack the navigation system."

"We have him in custody now. I was going to talk to him. I just wanted to make sure you were alright first," Aries said.

"That's so sweet of you, Aries. Thank you. Would you mind if I watched you interrogate him from behind the glass?" Vine asked.

"Not at all," Aries said.

The Broken Kingdom of Orion

Elenora stepped forward. "Can I come too? Like a support person for Vine," she asked. Aries nodded and he led the two girls to the interrogation room.

"Aries is so sweet. You're lucky to have him as a dad. He's kind, and caring, and cute," Vine told Elenora.

"Are you in love with him?" Elenora asked. Vine turned red.

"No! He was just there for me when Jax broke up with me. And he listened and gave me ice cream. He really cared about my feelings and that's sweet. Men aren't like that these days," she said. They watched as Aries entered the room with Jax. "I don't know why you would say something like that."

"Well, you know what they say. A shoulder to cry on is a dick to ride on. Plus, you're practically throwing yourself at him," Elenora said. Aries looked at the glass.

"I'm not trying to sleep with your dad, Elenora," Vine snapped.

"Hey, if you push the button next to the red light it turns your mic off," Aries said. Elenora's eyes widened in horror when she realized that Aries had heard them talking about him like that. She put her face in her hands in embarrassment as Vine glared at her.

"Way to go, Elenora," she muttered.

"You can't blame me for noticing that you're in love with Aries," Elenora said.

"I am not in love with Aries!" Vine yelled. Aries left the interrogation room and entered the room behind the glass.

"It's this button," he said as he turned off their mic. He left the room again after that.

"I need you to stop talking to me. You're being a terrible support person right now," Vine said to Elenora. Elenora agreed and the two watched Aries interrogate Jax.

Reji Ex

"Why are you trying to get the ship to crash on Ceres?" Aries asked.

Jax scoffed. "I don't have to tell you anything."

"That's fine. I don't have to let you off the ship in a cruiser. Could just be you by yourself in the frozen vacuum of space."

"Yeah, my point exactly. You don't see how that sounds? You're threatening my life because I don't agree with you," Jax snapped.

"Do you know what's on Ceres? It's an execution prison camp. Everyone on this ship would be executed, and that includes you," Aries said.

"No, the queen is there. She'd protect me. The same way she sent me to protect Elenora," Jax said with a smirk.

"She what?"

"Oh yeah. She knew where you hid Elenora the entire time. She told me everything I needed to know to protect Elenora from you," Jax said. Aries looked back at the glass for a moment. His mind immediately thought of the necklace that the General gave to Elenora. He said it was a homing device to call him if she was ever in trouble.

But what if that wasn't the case and it was a signal jammer to get the navigation to go to Ceres instead of Eris.

"Is The General a part of her plan?" he asked.

"The General? He was an official elective from Earth. Hired after the incident to reform Area 51. The queen has never met him," Jax said. Aries was relieved at that. He knew Elenora thought of the man like a father and the idea of him causing trouble would upset her.

"I know what your plan is. I just don't know why you have to involve Elenora."

The Broken Kingdom of Orion

"She's special. She belongs to the queen," Jax said. Aries glared at Jax.

"What do you think I'm doing?" Aries asked.

"Trying to overthrow the queen, your first victim. We all know you kidnapped her and forced her into marriage. She's uniting the galaxy and you're killing anyone that serves her. You're a monster. Just like how you killed your whole planet because she escaped," Jax accused. Aries leaned back in his chair.

"And how does Elenora tie into my evil plan exactly?" he asked.

"Manipulate a mother using her own child. Obviously," Jax said smugly.

"Sure, that makes sense. Manipulate her to do what?"

"It doesn't matter. I did my job and delivered Elenora back to the queen. As promised," Jax said.

"What are you talking about?" Aries asked. Jax leaned over the table.

"Turns out I didn't need the navigation system at all. I just needed to disconnect the autopilot. We were already going past Ceres. Just had to get close enough to the gravitational pull," Jax said. Aries stood up and left the room in a rush. He made his way to the captain's deck with Elenora and Vine quickly following behind him.

"Is he telling the truth? Are we going past Ceres?" Elenora asked.

"Yes, I just hope he wasn't telling the truth about shutting off the autopilot."

"What about the crew? Surely, they would have noticed if it was off, right?"

"Also, I just want to throw out that I don't want to sleep with you," Vine said.

Reji Ex

"We've moved past that, but okay." Aries was about to open the door to the captain's deck when the whole ship shifted. "Shit. We're falling," Aries said.

"What?" Elenora said.

"We fell into a gravitational pull. We're falling," Aries repeated. He entered the captain's deck and started shouting orders. Elenora turned and started running back down the hall.

"Where are you going?" Vine shouted.

"I have to find Marko. I'm sorry." Elenora ran to her room where Marko and Roman were.

"Elenora, what's happened?" Marko asked.

"We're falling to Ceres. Aries says it's-"

"It's a prison planet and we're all dead if we get captured. Yeah. we know," Roman said. Roman looked out the window at the planet rapidly approaching when he got an idea in his head. Roman chuckled slightly. "Hey Marko. Random question. You're married now. Can you promise me that you'll name your first-born son after me?"

"What? How can you ask that right now?" Marko said.

"Just promise, okay?"

"Okay, I promise. Whatever. What are we gonna do?" Marko asked. Roman started to walk out of the room.

"Do nothing. I trust Aries to right the course," he said before leaving. Roman walked down the hall and into a heavily populated room. "Hey, crewmen. I have a question. Would you say your loyalty to Aries is forever?"

"What are you talking about?" someone asked.

"Well, I'll just jump to the chase. Want to join a suicide mission with me?"

The Broken Kingdom of Orion

Roman and a group of crewmen quickly made their way to one of the escape pods. They dispersed from the ship. Predictably, someone from Ceres's communication tower tried to contact them.

"Surrender now. You're going to get captured. We have ships after you right now," they said.

"We're not going to surrender! You'll never take out the great Captain Aries," Roman responded.

"I'm not kidding. This is your last chance," communications said.

"Yeah, tell Queen Nava to go fuck herself," Roman replied. With that, the small ship was shot down and crashed into the planet below.

Aries got the Battleship stable and the autopilot turned back just in time to see the escape pod being shot out of the sky.

"Who took the escape pod?" Aries asked. A crewman typed on his computer to see whose access card opened the escape pod's doors.

"Roman was the last person to use an escape pod, captain," he said. Aries leaned back in his chair and closed his eyes. Roman must have figured that the Battleship would draw out guards to come and apprehend them. If there was a distraction ship or decoy, then they'd have a chance to escape.

"Okay, we have to go. We can't let his sacrifice be for nothing," Aries said.

"Yes sir," the crew answered.

"Sir, I have confirmation that another escape pod was used. A solo one," a woman said. Aries looked at her.

"Who took it?"

"There was no name attached but the video shows that Earth kid getting in it. The Helixian," she answered.

Reji Ex

"That son of a bitch escaped." Aries got up and left the deck as his crew sailed them away from Ceres.

16: Ceres's Prison

Roman and the group were quickly apprehended from the crash site. No one suffered major injuries, but they all knew that it didn't matter as guards dragged them to jail cells.

"Where's your captain?" a guard demanded.

"Oh, that would be me," Roman said.

"No. Aries. Where is Aries?"

"What, you didn't think we'd bring him. Did you?" Roman and the crew laughed at the guard. The guard growled in frustration and slapped Roman across the face. "Aries is safe, and everyone here has already agreed that we would rather die than give him up. So go ahead and do whatever you want to us, you're never getting Aries."

The guard studied Roman for a second.

"I know you," he said. Roman began to grow nervous. The crew knew about his past working for the queen, but it was never something that he talked about or was truly happy about. The guard smirked at him.

"Roman Florian of Kuiper. Trusted right hand of Queen Nava. Right? The queen had something special put in place for you. You're coming with us," the guard said. He opened the cage of Roman's cell,

Reji Ex

and two guards grabbed him by the arms and dragged him away. Every time he tried to catch his footing to be able to walk behind them, he'd get jerked and trip. After a few failed attempts at walking, he just let them drag him.

"This is not going to be fun for me is it?" Roman was dragged into a room and strapped into a chair. Two beautiful women entered the room and Roman groaned in defeat.

"Robots? I don't even get actual people to torture me?"

"It is an honor to serve our queen," the two women said in unison. Roman rolled his eyes.

"I know, robot ladies, I know." He leaned his head back in the chair and stared at the ceiling. "Let's get this over with."

The robots laid their hands on Roman's chest and sent a jolt of electricity through him. He jumped but didn't make a sound.

"It is an honor to serve our queen," they repeated. Roman looked at one of the guards, observing.

"Is repeating themselves the torture? Because that's gonna get old," he said.

"This isn't torture. You're just here to resubmit to the queen, then you can go back to your cell," the guard said. The robots shocked him again with a higher charge and repeated their line.

"This isn't gonna work. I follow Aries now. You know what's great about Aries? He doesn't have you blow up planets," Roman quipped.

"If that's how you feel, then it'll just be a slow and painful death for you," the guard said, injecting something into Roman's neck.

"What did you just do?" Roman demanded.

"It's a special tonic designed for you specifically. Just relax and let it work," he said. Roman didn't have much of a memory of the next events. He remembered being shocked repeatedly and the bots repeating their line over and over. He remembered at some point he was screaming, and his vision had blurred. He felt a warm, gentle hand touch his face. A robot smiled down at him. He was taken aback by the beautiful face the robot was wearing. He leaned into the warm hand.

"We don't want you to suffer. You know what to do to make it stop. Please make your suffering stop," the robot whispered.

"I can't betray Aries," Roman muttered. He was shocked again until he passed out. A bucket of water was thrown on him to wake him up.

"What's going on?" Roman asked. The guard just laughed and the shock torture resumed.

"Stop fighting, Roman. You're worth more to the queen alive than you are dead," the guard said. Roman was out of breath. His mouth was dry, and his throat was sore from screaming. He didn't even remember what was going on or how he got there. He remembered the sacrifice he made to make sure Aries and his crew got away safely.

Why did he do that? What did he owe Aries? Oh right, Aries was the one who reunited him with his brother.

"My brother!" Roman said. The guard smirked.

"We know about him. We know about his crimes. We know that you sold your soul to the queen to exempt him from punishment. You can't keep fighting this," the guard said.

"You'll kill my brother if I don't submit, won't you," Roman said. The guard shrugged.

"It's up to the queen. She's killed for less," he said.

"So you know she's on the wrong side?"

Reji Ex

"Do you want to keep your baby brother safe or not?"

"Yes," Roman said, looking down.

"What do you say," the guard taunted. Roman sighed.

"It's an honor to..." his voice trailed off as his mind went somewhere else. He was dreaming that he was back on Kuiper. He and Marko were safe and living free as children, before the bad things started happening.

"You're awful to me, Roman. Why can't you act like a real big brother," Marko would say to him. At the time, Roman would laugh at his little brother being so upset by whatever prank he just pulled.

"This is what big brothers do," Roman would reply.

Years later, their planet was being taken over by the queen's forces.

"Please, my brother is just a kid. He didn't know what he was doing. He's just a kid. I'm begging you," Roman was on his hands and knees, begging the royal guards to let Marko go. The guards smirked at him.

"You're willing to do anything to protect your little brother?" they asked.

"What do you mean?" Roman asked.

"We'll send your brother to a...let's say a little camp, to keep him safe. And you will come work for her royal highness," a guard said. Roman reluctantly nodded in agreement.

"Roman? Where are they taking me? Where are they taking you?" young Marko asked his brother. Roman tried to get to his brother but the guard kept them apart.

"It's okay, Marko. This...this is what brothers do," he said. The guards pulled him onto his feet and led him to a ship.

The Broken Kingdom of Orion

"While you're here you only need to know three things: number one, we worship the queen. Number two, the pirate Aries is a crazed murderer, and we must stop him at all costs. And number three, your soul belongs to the queen. If you ever betray her, best pray that she doesn't find you. Got that?"

Roman quickly rose in rank. He followed the three rules as if his life depended on it. In his mind, his life did depend on it. His brother's life was on the line. At any point, the queen's army could raid the camp that they had sent Marko to. He used his rank to find the camp that the queen was sending the children to. It was on Earth, but he didn't have time to use this information before he was given an assignment.

"You're being sent to Helix to deliver a present!" the queen told Roman over a video call.

"The present…the present that…" Roman couldn't even say what he was thinking. The queen nodded.

"That's the one!" she said cheerfully.

"You removed the children from Helix. Right?" Roman asked. The queen looked distantly and then back to Roman.

"Mhmm. The people of Helix used to live in my mother and father's kingdom, so they should follow my rule, but they don't," she said. It wasn't until Roman was on Battleship Juniper that he learned she hadn't removed the children before having the planet blown up. He learned that she was never interested in the safety of children like he was led to believe.

Aries did care for children. Aries never lied to him. Aries never threatened his brother's life. Aries was Roman's savior from the tyrant queen.

Reji Ex

Roman suddenly had visions of choking the life out of Aries. He imagined Aries's silver eyes widening in fear with his hands wrapped firmly around his neck, the color draining from his already pale face and the light flickering out. He heard that Orions had blue blood, and suddenly, the idea of stabbing Aries and watching him bleed out, painting the ground blue, enticed him.

Roman felt himself begin to tremble in fear at the visions he was having against his will. He knew Aries. Aries was going to save the galaxy from the queen. Aries was a hero. *Aries had to die.*

Roman jerked awake. He looked around and realized he was in a prison cell. "Hey. You alright man?" someone asked. Roman sat up, and as soon as he did, he felt his stomach shift. He leaned over and emptied the contents of his stomach onto the floor beside him. When he was finished, he leaned against the wall. He couldn't remember what happened. He remembered the vivid, horrible dream he had but everything else was a blur. He vaguely remembered being shocked as a form of punishment for his betrayal. He shuddered at the thought of killing his new captain.

"What happened to me?" Roman asked. He tried to keep his voice from trembling, but he was unsuccessful.

"I don't know. A couple guards dragged your body in and threw you in your cell like a ragdoll. I thought you were dead," the crewman said. Roman looked around his small room. Three walls were entirely cemented over but at the entrance of the cell were bars. He had a small cot in the corner next to him and an empty bucket in the other corner. There was a bucket of water next to the door but nothing else was in the room.

The Broken Kingdom of Orion

"The crew is safe. For now. The suicide mission worked. Aries was able to get away. But he's Aries. He's gonna come back for us," the crewman said.

"You really think that?" Roman asked, looking up at him. This was the first time Roman noticed that the crewman wasn't in his cell but in the cell across from him.

"I do. I know Aries. I have followed him since the beginning. He won't leave us behind. Unlike…someone else," he said. Roman bitterly knew that he meant the queen, who used lives as stepping stones to get to her goal, which was currently unknown.

Orion, gone. Helix, gone. Eris, captured. Kuiper, captured. Makemake, captured. And why? There wasn't a rhyme or reason behind her vicious takeover.

"Aries can't come here. They will kill him," Roman said.

"Of course, I know that. He knows that too. That's not something he's worried about, though. Maybe with the return of the princess, he should worry more about his own life, but he will still come back for us. It's who he is."

Reji Ex

17: Battleship Juniper

Aries sat in his captain's chair as the battleship flew away from Ceres. He was thinking about his daughter. He wanted more than anything to form a relationship with her. He had 20 years to make up for. Unfortunately for him, he wouldn't be able to. He stood up and walked to the communications room.

"Out! Everybody, out. Now," he ordered. The crew up and left with a, "Yes, captain."

Aries sat at a radio station and stared blankly for a moment. *Was he really about to do this?* He knew it was the right thing to do. He knew this would solve a lot of problems. But Elenora would be devastated. He wouldn't ever get to know her the way a dad knows their daughter, and she wouldn't get to know him.

Aries typed into the computer to set the radio signal. He held the mic in his hands. There was no turning back if he did this, but he had to do the right thing. He pressed the button.

"I want to speak to Nava," he said into the mic. There was silence for a minute.

Aries's heart beat loudly as he waited for a response.

"Her majesty is here. Speak your message," a reply said.

The Broken Kingdom of Orion

"I want you to let them go, Nava. All of them. I want them to be let go and unharmed," Aries said.

"Why would I ever do that?" a woman said over the radio. He knew it was her.

She was there and heard his request. He swallowed hard before sealing his fate. "Because I'll surrender. I'll surrender if you let my crew go." There was another pause before Aries heard her response.

"I like that deal. I'll have their ship repaired too, just because I'm so nice. I'll see you soon, Dante," Nava said. Aries clicked the radio off and walked out of the room. The radio crew was waiting outside.

"Back to work," Aries ordered. The crew rushed back into the room as Aries walked away. He didn't want to see Elenora before leaving. He'd change his mind if he saw her. He had a group of loyal followers willing to die for him. He couldn't abandon them in their time of need. Aries made his way to the bay. He entered his code into the door of a solo ship. He flew the ship to Ceres and landed outside of the prison building.

A group of guards and robots met him with guns aimed at him. Aries held out his arms and a guard put handcuffs on him. More chains were added to restrain him. He rolled his eyes. He was unarmed but they didn't care. He needed to be seen as more of a threat than he was. He held his head high as the guards let him to his inevitable death. He was okay with this.

Meanwhile, Roman sat at the back of his cell sipping his cup of water slowly to not cause more stomach upset. The crewman that was talking to him leaned against the bars to see Roman. Roman did not care for the conversation and just wanted to rest, but he didn't tell this to the crewman.

"Where did they take you?" the crewman asked.

Reji Ex

"To get a little zappy zap. Non-harming torture for my disloyalty to the crown," Roman said bitterly.

"Were you that important to the queen that she needed to teach you a lesson?" he asked. Roman shrugged and sipped his water.

"I guess so. Or maybe she just hates betrayal even from her pawns. I didn't think I was all that special," Roman said. The sound of the old iron door swinging open made Roman flinch. The crewman looked at who entered and his face paled.

"Captain?" he muttered. Roman dropped his cup and jumped up to the edge of his cell. Sure enough, a couple of guards led in Aries who was entirely chained up as if he were a major threat.

"Captain, what's going on here?"

Aries stared straight ahead without looking at his crew or saying a word to them.

"Aries? What's happening?" Roman shouted. He reached out of the bars to try to grab Aries, but he was led away too quickly. More guards poured in as Aries neared the end of the hallway. They unlocked cells and roughly grabbed the crew. Roman fought against the guard that grabbed him to try to reach his captain.

"Aries?! Aries, what did you do?" he shrieked. Aries looked over his shoulder to make eye contact with Roman. That one look sent shivers down Roman's spine as he realized what was happening. He let the guard drag him out. The rest of the crew were shouting in confusion all the way back to their ship. The guards pushed the prisoners towards the ship and demanded that they get on it and leave.

"What just happened?" someone asked when they were safely away from Ceres.

"Isn't it obvious? Aries traded his life for ours," Roman said.

"He can't do that. That's not…that's not what I thought he was gonna do," the crewman that had been speaking to Roman before said. Roman shrugged and took the pilot's seat.

"Since when do you know how to fly?" he asked.

"What? I was literally a ship captain before I was captured by Aries. You know this!" Roman flew the ship back to the Battleship Juniper. Roman connected to the communications room to request landing.

"Who did you say you were?" the communications tower asked. Roman groaned in frustration.

"It's Roman, returning from the suicide mission," he said.

"You know how that doesn't add up?"

"Okay, Cynthia. Grant us access, and I will explain it better in person," Roman said.

"I can't grant access without permission from the captain. You know this," Cynthia replied to him. Roman stared at the battleship for a moment.

"Aries is no longer with us. You're gonna need to speak with the princess if you want the next person in line," Roman said. Cynthia spoke with Elenora. This was the first time that she heard about Roman's sacrifice and coincidentally, Aries's. Roman was granted permission to enter the bay and the crew went back to their normal jobs on the battleship.

Roman was staring out the window at the shrinking planet in the distance when Elenora and Marko found him. His brother encased him in a hug.

"What happened back there?" he asked.

"Oh, the usual. I got punished for infidelity and then Aries sacrificed himself for the entire crew," Roman mumbled.

Reji Ex

"What?" Elenora demanded.

"Why would he do that?" Marko asked. Roman looked him in the eyes.

"Because, as I've told you, Aries's loyalty is undying. He protects innocent lives," Roman said. His normal, nonchalant, jokey attitude towards his brother was replaced with a harsh tone. Marko took a step back; he'd never seen his brother angry toward him. Roman turned and started walking away. "I have to go to the infirmary. I was electrocuted."

He walked to the infirmary where Besnik immediately spotted him and got him a bed. Besnik and Roman had gotten close over the past month, since they were captured by Aries. They spent a lot of their time together before Roman found Marko.

"I was worried about you," Besnik said.

"I'm fine. I was shocked a couple of times but…I don't know. I just wanted you to give me a check-up to make sure everything's working right," Roman said. Besnik looked at him and smirked.

"You wanted me to do it. Like, specifically?" Besnik asked, gathering his equipment to check over Roman's vitals. He started by listening to Roman's heart.

"Well, you're the only one I trust right now. Aries is dead," Roman said. Besnik paused in surprise before checking Roman's blood pressure.

"He is?" he questioned.

"He will be. He sacrificed…" Roman started but his voice trailed off. He looked away from Besnik. Besnik took his face in his hands to check his pupil's reaction.

"Are you…are you crying?" Besnik asked. Roman shrugged.

The Broken Kingdom of Orion

"I've made so many mistakes in my life. But he trusted me, even if he didn't admit it. I trusted him. I… I didn't think he actually cared about me that much. I never expected him to give his life to save me, you know."

"I care about you that much," Besnik replied, trying to comfort Roman.

"I never wanted to hurt anyone. I'm sorry for blowing up your planet. If I could be defiant to the queen now, I should have started back then," Roman said.

"It's never too late to become better. I mean, look at me. When I first got here, I was a trembling ball of anxiety personified. Now, I'm almost a doctor," Besnik said with a slight laugh.

"I think I'll always be subpar," Roman said.

"Well, that's not true. You're a really brave guy. You worked your way up the ranks to being a captain," Besnik said. Roman scoffed.

"I blew up your planet because of that."

"If it's any consolation, I had no family or friends. I was just focused on surviving." Besnik looked away for a moment, thinking about his old life back on Helix. Roman could relate to that. His family was killed and he only had his brother left. Everyone had a better life before the queen messed things up. Roman looked at Besnik.

"That's something great about you, though. You're resourceful, and smart, and capable of surviving. Any woman would be lucky to have you. You'll make your own family and live the rest of your life on another planet, safe, somewhere," Roman said.

"Oh…Ummm, no women actually." Besnik looked down, sheepishly.

Reji Ex

"What do you mean? Oh, I see," Roman replied, realizing what Besnik meant. He couldn't help but smile to himself a little bit at Besnik's confession. He wasn't sure he'd ever find love for himself, but Besnik seemed to balance him. He was quiet and rational whereas Roman was constantly joking and being annoying. Roman wasn't quite sure what his sexuality was. When he was a kid he thought he knew but his dad didn't like it so he just figured he'd be alone forever to keep his father happy. But his father was gone now and he felt comfortable with Besnik. Roman wasn't quite sure that he knew what love was or how it felt, but he knew being near Besnik felt right. He felt like he could be himself.

Besnik and Roman stared at each other for a split moment before Besnik cleared his throat. "Your vitals look good, except you could use a saline drip for dehydration."

He got an IV catheter out of a nearby drawer.

"Do you trust me?" he asked Roman. Roman touched Besnik's face.

"Do you trust me?" he asked him back.

Besnik turned Roman's arm and placed the IV in one swift motion. He retrieved a bag of saline and hooked it up to Roman's catheter.

"I'll come back and check on you in an hour to see how you're feeling," he said before turning. Roman grabbed his hand. Besnik felt a jolt of electricity wave through him and turned to face Roman.

"I do trust you," he said. Besnik closed the distance between them and gently placed his lips on Roman's. Roman returned the kiss with electrifying passion.

"I have…I have other patients I need to check on," Besnik said as he pulled away.

The Broken Kingdom of Orion

"Well, I sure hope you don't treat them the same way you treated me," Roman teased. Besnik rolled his eyes and left the area.

On the other side of the ship, Elenora was whipping through the hallways. Crewmen were at every corner, whispering about their captain's brave sacrifice. A few stopped Elenora when they saw her.

"What do we do now?"

"Who's our captain? Whose orders do we follow?"

"Are we abandoning Aries?"

"No, I…I don't know…" Elenora stammered. She looked to Marko who looked just as lost as she did. Elenora was a timid and shy girl, but that didn't matter to any of these people who were looking to her to lead them.

"We need to make a plan?" she said, questioning herself. She didn't have a plan. She didn't have any idea how to make one. But the mention of plan-making seemed to start to put the crewmen at ease, so she continued.

"A small team will be put together to go back for Aries, but we have to be stealthy about it. Right? They'll be expecting us to go back for him. We need to plan but…we can't take too long to act," she stated. The crew nodded in agreement.

"Sounds good to me, new captain," one said.

"Oh, no. I'm not a leader," she replied.

"You are today, Elenora," another said. Elenora dismissed herself from the group and continued down the halls. Marko followed her closely. They met up with Vine, who was in the computer room.

"I heard what happened to Aries," she said without looking up from the computer.

"What are you doing?" Elenora asked.

Reji Ex

"I assumed you were here to invite me on the rescue mission, too. I'm looking into Ceres a little bit more. The whole planet is only the size of New York. It's uninhabited except for the prison. Those robot ladies that Marko told us about will likely be there, and I think I can hack into their system if I'm careful enough," Vine said.

"Then what happens after you hack their system?" Marko asked.

"Well, we can make them our killing machines instead of hers."

"Wait, you want to kill people?" Marko asked, horrified.

"Yes, Marko. What did you think was gonna happen? We go to Ceres, ask nicely for Aries back, and sing kumbaya around a campfire? No. We go in, guns blazing, and we empty mags until we save Aries," Vine said.

"He's not going to sleep with you just because you go on a killing rampage for him," Marko said bitterly. Vine got up and slapped him in the face.

"Guys, cut it out! We don't have time to fight each other. We are literally in the middle of a war right now," Elenora scolded.

"I'm not going to sleep with my best friend's dad just because I'm attracted to him. Yes, I sleep around when I'm not with someone but I have self control. I want you guys to stop slut shaming me about it," Vine snapped.

"And I know we're in a war, but I don't want to kill anyone. I've done enough killing. Killing ruined my life," Marko said. Elenora whipped around to look at her husband.

"What do you mean by that?" she asked. Marko sighed and sat in a chair.

"I was twelve," he started.

"Twelve? You were murdering people when you were twelve?" Vine questioned.

The Broken Kingdom of Orion

"Was Kuiper a violent planet?" Elenora asked.

"No, the queen…" Marko started but he stopped and pushed his hands into his head. Elenora wrapped her arms around him.

"You can tell us," she whispered to him.

"I went home and they were dead," he whispered.

"Who?" Vine asked, suddenly concerned about her friend. Marko looked at the two before him.

"My parents. They were shot, and I don't even know why. I saw them on the ground, and I just grabbed something. I didn't even know what it was, but I smashed it against the soldier's head over and over again. I saw the fear in his eyes before his face got covered in blood. Roman pulled me off of him and…and more soldiers came in. Next thing I knew, I was on Earth and I never saw my brother again," Marko recalled.

"Until now," Elenora added.

"Yeah," he said. He hugged his wife as if he was protecting himself from the memories. "I just don't want to hurt anybody. Hasn't there been enough death?"

"You know she's going to kill Aries if we don't do something. Those robots are hackable, and I can take out the actual human guards with them," Vine explained.

"I don't want to be involved," Marko said.

"This must be really triggering for you," Vine said.

Marko looked at her and nodded. "I'm sorry for what I said. It was uncalled for. I just…I can't do this. I'm sorry."

"We might not even need you. I mean, we have to have a small team anyways to decrease the risk of getting caught. You could just stay back," Elenora said.

Reji Ex

"Yeah, I mean, we need a pilot, so I assume Roman is on board," Vine said. "Definitely need a medic. Probably Doc since he's more experienced. And me, obviously, cause robots."

"It's my father and my idea, so I'm going," Elenora said. Marko sighed and rubbed his face.

"Well, if you're going then I'm going to keep you safe." Elenora hugged him and he bared his head on her shoulder.

"Thank you, Marko," Elenora whispered.

Marko kissed the top of her head. "He's gonna be okay. He has a daughter like you protecting him," Marko said softly. The three of them shared a knowing look. Then silently made their way down the hall to get their rescue mission started.

18: Ceres's Prison

Aries' arms were chained to the wall, and his legs were chained to the ground. He scoffed at how ridiculously overkill this was. He was unarmed and completely defenseless, and they go and act like he could kill with a single glare. He felt sad for his crew but was happy knowing they were long gone. He didn't plan for any of them to remain loyal. He gave them their freedom, and they were free to go. No one would be coming for him, and that was okay.

The door to his prison opened and *she* glided in. Her flowing gown was red and gold like the one she wore when they first met. Her long brown hair was tied up in a bun that sat at the top of her head. Her green, cat-like eyes were focused on Aries with amusement. She smiled with her fangs showing. Aries's heart fluttered for a second, but then he remembered why she was there, not to save him, but to inflict torture directly.

"It's really you, Dante," she said with a smile. She placed his face in her hands to study it better. "You're older than I remembered. You know, when I heard that stupid pseudo name, I was worried if it wasn't you."

Reji Ex

"Hello, Nava," Aries said calmly as if he were meeting an old friend at a coffee shop.

"I can't wait to have fun with you. I've dreamed of things I wanted to try. So many options." Nava ripped at Aries's shirt to expose his chest.

"That was my favorite shirt, Nava."

"Then you shouldn't have worn it when you turned yourself in, Dante," she retorted. "I don't want to do too much damage to your gorgeous body, but I also want this to hurt. I'm definitely not doing any permanent damage to that face. Hmm, kind of limits my options here."

"If this monologuing is part of the torture, it's working. Please kill me before you continue," Aries taunted.

"Oh, that's so cute," Nava said before swiftly punching him in the stomach. Aries gasped and coughed as the wind got knocked out of him. He didn't remember her being that strong before. "I hope you are well rested because you're never sleeping again until you die. And that's not hyperbole, I'm planning on killing you. Hopefully in front of your new girlfriend. I think that'll be fun."

Aries thought for a moment and laughed.

"Do you already need another lesson about mocking me?" Nava questioned.

"The only girl I've been around lately is Elenora," Aries said.

Nava blinked. She wasn't expecting Aries to find her. "Oh…even better. How humiliating for you to have your daughter watch you die." Nava snapped her fingers, and two robots came in and stared at Aries.

The Broken Kingdom of Orion

"You would do that to your own daughter?" Aries asked. The robots took turns hitting Aries with mallets. Nava shrugged while she watched Aries take hit after hit.

"Doesn't matter much to me. Hopefully, she'll see how weak you are and join my cause. If not, then I'll just kill her," she said. Aries jerked sharply at his chains. He almost got his arm off the wall as he did. The sharp movement caused the robots to jump back, but Nava just giggled. "Did that upset you? Dante, I expected better from you. Already showing me your weak spot. What? That stupid girl of yours is special somehow?"

"She's our daughter!" Aries yelled.

Aries slumped on his chains. Blue blood ran down his arm from being cut into by the chains. He didn't seem to notice, but Nava did and smiled.

"I just love Orion blood. Blue is such a pretty color when it's splattered all over the place, don't you think so?" She walked over to Aries and licked a drip off of his arm. He flinched from her, not expecting her to do something so creepy. Suddenly, with the conversation and the look she gave him when she tasted his blood, he began to fear for his life. He knew she was planning on killing him, but this was somehow different.

"I wonder if Eliza's blood is blue too," she mocked.

"Elenora," Aries corrected. Nava clicked her tongue. Aries looked at her and then looked away. "Is she…"

"Oh, ask what you were going to ask. Don't pretend to be shy about it now," Nava said. Aries looked up at her with sincerity.

"Nava, please, tell me the truth. Is she mine?" he asked. Nava shivered and smiled.

"I like it when you beg. Do it again," she demanded.

Reji Ex

"Please," Aries said. He let his head slump down. "I'm begging you. Is Elenora my daughter?"

"Aww, that is so sweet. What do I get in return? Why should I honor this request?" Nava asked. Aries looked up at her with pleading eyes. "Oh, I know! Two days: no food, no water, no sleep. The only interaction you'll ever have is these two poking you with cattle prods and beating you senseless. What do you say?"

"I...deal," Aries muttered.

"Wow, you don't even know if I'll tell the truth or not. It'll torture you forever. I could lie. You know I'm good at sneaking lies past you and you did all this for nothing. Oh well." Nava smiled.

"I really did love you, you know," Aries muttered. Nava was suddenly filled with rage. She turned on Aries and punched him as hard as she could in the face. He yelped in pain. He felt his nose crack and blood began dripping down.

"Oh no, your pretty face," Nava said before turning on her heels and leaving.

Aries was left with the two bots that changed their hands from mallets to tasers. He closed his eyes.

"For Elenora," he thought to himself before the shocks began.

A few hours later, the robots finally powered down. Aries weakly looked around the room. This was most definitely a trap for him to fall asleep. He knew as soon as he did there would be something cruel to wake him up. But he couldn't help it. It was the first time in hours that he wasn't being hit, and his body was beginning to relax. His eyes grew heavy. He just needed a second to rest. As soon as he started to drift, the robots summoned a loud blaring siren as well as flashing lights. He yelped when he was startled awake. Then, the robots quieted again.

This went on for the entirety of what Aries thought was night. His chest was covered in bruises and swelling. He figured there wasn't any way that they could beat him on the second day without causing serious harm to his internal organs. They surprised him by hitting him gentler in the bruised, swollen places. Just enough to aggravate his already injured body but not enough to cause new wounds. Then, of course, the shocks. He noticed that the area where they chose to shock him was beginning to burn. His flesh was turning black under the taser. With each jolt, he began losing feeling in his fingertips as well as the location of skin that was being seared off.

"This is for Elenora," he thought to himself.

As the third day began, Nava waltzed back into the room as if nothing had happened.

"Good morning, Dante," she said in a cheerful voice. He rolled his head up to look at her but was already starting to be too weak to do even that much.

"I was thinking that today I would whip you, then by tomorrow your followers should be here for the show. I'm thinking about a live fire range?" she said.

"Please…" Aries gasped out weakly.

"Oh right. That stupid promise. Again, I want to point out that you have way too much trust that I'll even be honest. I might even lie and say that she's not yours but the butler's, just to upset you and make you give up quicker," Nava said. Aries found the strength to snap his head up. Nava faked a gasp. "Oops did I just confess? Well, guess there's no use hiding it. Congratulations, Dante. It's a girl."

Aries smiled while Nava glared at him. She had no intention of lying about Elenora's parental lineage. She knew that the truth would perk him up, but she wasn't expecting him to be completely rejuvenated. She wanted to break him completely before ending him once and for all.

"Ready to get whipped?" she asked. Aries nodded and it fueled Nava's anger.

She wasn't asking his permission. She didn't need his consent to hurt him. The bots unchained Aries, turning him to expose his back. Nava ripped his shirt the rest of the way off and held out her hand. A robot quickly retrieved a whip for her. She began to whip deep cuts into Aries's back. He tried to hold back a scream with each hit because he knew that was what she wanted.

"Scream, Dante. I want to know I'm causing you pain," she demanded. She whipped him again, but he clenched his teeth to avoid making noise. "Scream, or I swear, I will force you to lay on a slab of salt."

Nava eventually shrieked in frustration over Aries' silence. She clenched her fists, and letting him drop to the ground. She pinned him down and punched him in the face repeatedly, not stopping until she saw that he was beginning to pass out. She nodded to the robots who did, in fact, drag in a slab of salt. The robots lowered the slab onto his bleeding back. Aries gasped at the stinging pain that the salt caused but was unable to do much else due to the pressure that the heavy slab was causing on his lungs. He had barely enough movement to inhale painful breaths. The salt irritated his open wounds, and the weight was beginning to suffocate him. Nava crouched down so she was closer to Aries's eye level on the floor.

"When I say scream, you scream. Got it? Or your lungs get crushed. Is this fun for you? Is it fun to disrespect your queen?" Nava asked. Aries shook his head. Nava snapped her fingers, and the slab was removed. Aries took a breath of air that filled his lungs. He laid his head on the floor for a moment of comfort and rest. Nava flipped him over so he was on his back. She looked into his deep silver eyes. She took a deep breath, and her anger was replaced with something else. Her sadistic mind and her feelings from the past stirred lust inside her. Her ex-husband was helpless before her and she loved to inflict pain and torture, even mental torture. She bit her lip and smirked at Aries.

"I want to offer another trade," she said softly. He looked at her in fear. "You're just so worried about that daughter of yours. I can make you a deal for her safety."

"What do you want?" Aries asked.

Nava traced her hand down his chest. "Something. You don't even have to do anything but lay there, completely still." Nava's hands made their way to the top of Aries's pants and he began to panic.

"No, no I don't want this," he protested with newly found adrenaline.

"Sure, you do," Nava said as she began to slip him out of his pants and work him. "This is all you have to do to ensure her safety."

"Please, don't do this," he begged. She left dark bruises and bites along his chest and stomach as she lowered her mouth to taste him, savoring the sound of him begging her to stop.

"Don't you want your little princess to be safe?" she asked. Aries's eyes stared blankly at the ceiling. He nodded wordlessly. She climbed on top of him and straddled his hips. She stared down at him. "Then say it."

"You can…you can do what you want to me." His voice trembled. "Please don't hurt Elenora."

Reji Ex

"Oh, Dante, you should have never let me know your weakness." Nava began to move onto him. He tried to close his eyes and imagine he was somewhere else, but Nava didn't like that. She gripped his face roughly, causing him to snap his eyes open and look at her. She dug her nails into his cheek as she forced a rough kiss on him. She stole her pleasure from him several times. Aries wanted it to end, but she wasn't stopping.

"Please, don't make me," he whispered as he realized what she wanted. She laughed at his begging and began to choke him. He was never into choking or consenting to pain, and she knew that. She gave an evil smirk down at him. His vision began to blur as he was losing air. Her actions were clear to him. Finish or I'll finish you. He arched his back as he plunged into her. She giggled and sunk her fangs into his neck. He screamed at the sudden pain and sacrificed what she was demanding.

She moaned one last time before getting up from him.

"See? That wasn't so bad now, was it?" she mocked. The first thing Aries did was immediately pull up his pants. He pushed himself into the corner of his prison cell and hugged himself. Nava laughed and rolled her eyes.

"Don't be so dramatic. I should keep you for myself. Fake your death and just keep you as my personal toy. You'd like that?" she said. Aries continued to stare blankly ahead. "I made a promise to kill you, though, so I guess I'll just have to end our love affair here."

"How gracious of you," Aries muttered. Nava acted like she didn't hear him. She turned and walked out, leaving Aries alone.

He felt used and violated. He looked at his wrists as they dripped his blue blood. He must have been fighting a lot more than he realized. His hand carefully felt around his neck. He was certain that

The Broken Kingdom of Orion

Nava left hand-shaped bruises there, but the bite was what worried him. It dripped with blood, and he knew if he survived this it would scar over—leaving some sort of claim over him. His face was beginning to swell where she beat him earlier. He didn't even want to think about what his back looked like, scored with a whip, then salt in his wounds.

The truth was, he still loved her. He loved her and he didn't understand why she wanted to inflict so much pain on him. He laid down on the cold, dirty floor. He began to shiver from the cold and pain. Why would she do this to him? What did she possibly have to gain from this? His heart hurt. He loved her. He wanted to have a normal happy life with her. All he could do was lay there and think, "why, why, why." No matter how much he loved her, no matter how much he gave her, no matter what he did, she would still hurt him one way or another. Why did he still love her after everything she put him through? What did he have to gain?

This was for Elenora's safety, he reminded himself. His daughter that he knew next to nothing about. And now he never will, because tomorrow Nava was going to slowly kill him. He never even got the chance to be called "dad" by his daughter. He lived a life full of regrets, but at least he'd die knowing the last thing he ever did was protect his daughter.

He didn't feel safe enough to fall asleep, even though he needed it. He stayed up and stared at the door, waiting for Nava to come in and hurt him again. He wished that she would just kill him already instead of toying with him.

The next morning, robots entered and handcuffed him. They led him into an arena where he knew Nava was planning on killing him.

She turned to see him as he approached. She smiled, and it sent shivers down his spine.

"Morning Dante! How did you sleep last night? I slept pretty great. I brought you here because our system has spotted a small craft headed this way. I will admit, I'm upset that it's not the whole team but we will make do with what we have, right?" She rambled. Aries was tied with his hands above his head and no other restraints. It was vastly different than before. He could easily twist out of this rope and run if he wanted to. But he realized that he actually couldn't. He felt entirely too weak, and his body was in too much pain to do much else. He leaned against the post that he was tied to.

"If you're gonna kill me, just get it over with" he muttered. His words slurred from the swelling in his face. He could barely see out of one eye— the other eye being completely swollen shut. There was a stabbing pain in his stomach, and he didn't know if it was from the starving, beating, or burning. His wrists ached as the rope was tied directly into his open wounds. He didn't want to give up. He didn't want to abandon Elenora like this, but he did what he could to secure her safety and that was enough for him.

Nava had set up a table about ten feet in front of Aries. The table had an array of guns, knives, maces, and other types of melee weapons. She traced her hand over each one while she decided which weapon to start with. She picked up a plasma gun and shifted it between her hands.

"Please keep in mind that this is for my entertainment, so this will be as long and drawn out as possible. Oh! And don't forget to scream so your friends know where to find you," Nava said. She raised her weapon. The plasma gun that she chose was specifically meant to be a warning shot weapon. This gun was not meant to kill anyone, but if shot enough with it, death was inevitable, like with anything else. The plasma gun shot a ball of considerate star plasma. It was a thick ball, much like a large airsoft pellet, that burnt the skin on impact. Nava cruelly aimed at the hickey marks she left the night before. As if she had made them purposefully to be targets. The first hit was on Aries's lower stomach. He whipped his head back as he got burnt and screamed.

"Perfect!' Nava beamed. "Now do that again until your little friends find you"

19: Outside of the Prison

The small rescue team, consisting of Elenora, Vine, Doc, Roman, and Marko, landed their carrier near the prison. Elenora was the first to rush out of the craft and into the building.

"Vine, shut down the bots while we find Aries," she ordered.

"I know what I'm doing," Vine replied. Elenora rushed off. Marko chased after her, worried that she'd get hurt or captured. Soon, he realized something that she didn't.

"Elenora, wait. Stop," he demanded.

"I can't stop," Elenora said.

"Just listen. This is a highly secured prison, but we haven't seen a single guard or bot," Marko said. Elenora stopped and looked around. They were deep within the prison now and he was right. It was as if they were the only people there. Doc and Roman were able to catch up to them.

"Why are we stopped?" Roman asked.

The Broken Kingdom of Orion

"This…this might be a trap," Elenora said. She didn't even have time to reconsider a plan before a pained scream echoed through the halls. "That was Aries!"

Elenora took off running in the direction that she thought she heard the scream come from. She stopped for a moment, unsure of which direction to head, when she heard a second scream and kept running. She suddenly found herself outside in a courtyard-like place. She squinted her eyes as they adjusted to the light. When her vision cleared, she saw the human and robot guards sitting in stadium seats surrounding the courtyard. She saw Aries, bloodied and beaten, tied to a pole. She saw Nava aiming a gun at her. Elenora stopped and held her hands up.

Nava shot at her, hitting her shoulder with a plasma ball. She screamed as her skin burned and knelt on the ground.

"Stop! We had a deal!" Aries shouted. Nava's eyes flickered between Aries and Elenora, and her mouth twisted into a sadistic smile.

"This is her?" Nava laughed, "She's not much. I wouldn't have traded what you did."

"Please," Aries begged Nava.

"Please what? Is there something you don't want her to know? Like how you whored yourself to me last night in a pathetic attempt to protect her? Is that some big secret? I think everyone knows you're a slut," Nava mocked.

"Stop it!" Elenora snapped.

"Oh, tell her, Dante. Tell her how it was the best part of your time here," Nava said with a laugh. Aries looked at his daughter, then hung his head in shame.

Reji Ex

Aries's embarrassment was suddenly replaced with red rage. As soon as he felt it, he realized it wasn't his emotion he was feeling. It was Elenora's.

In a flash, Elenora was at the table. She grabbed a spear and ran it into Nava's side, knocking her down and pinning her to the ground. Nava screamed, and for the first time in his life, Aries saw fear in Nava's eyes. Elenora growled as she kept pushing the spear into Nava. The pressure caused the spear to snap with the head of it firmly lodged into Nava's side.

Elenora turned the pole on its side and pushed it into Nava's neck, choking her. Nava looked into her daughter's eyes, but they were entirely clouded by her rage. She looked at Aries and reached out her hand as if begging him to untie himself to save her. Elenora looked up and noticed the guards had all drawn their guns and aimed them at her. She stood up with her hands in the air in surrender. Nava quickly darted off to safety, holding her side. The guards began to spring to action to arrest Elenora, but before any guard had a chance to do anything, the robots that sat beside them quietly had their eyes glow blue. The bots began killing all the guards in the stands.

"Nice touch with the blue eyes, Vine," Elenora muttered to herself. Elenora heard footsteps running up behind her. She grabbed her spear pole, ready to fight, but when she turned, she saw Marko, Doc, and Roman. Roman and Doc quickly ran to Aries and untied him. Aries collapsed into them as they helped lay him down.

"Damn, Captain, what did you get yourself into this time?" Doc teased.

"Date with the ex-wife," Aries joked back. Aries found himself quickly losing the adrenaline that has been keeping him going. His vision blurred, and black edges began to form around his line of sight.

The Broken Kingdom of Orion

"He's losing consciousness. We have to get him back to the ship," Roman said.

"Captain, can you still hear me? I need you to fight this. I need you to stay awake just a little longer," Doc instructed.

"El?" Aries mumbled weakly. Elenora went to his side and held his hand.

"I'm right here," she said.

"'M sorry," he slurred out.

"You don't have anything to be sorry for. Doc needs you to stay awake until you can get to the ship. You're gonna be okay," Elenora said. Aries' one unswollen eye slowly drifted closed. "Come on, dad, you have to stay awake."

Suddenly, his eye snapped back open and he focused on her.

"D'you jus call me dad?" he asked.

"Yeah, you're my dad, aren't you?" Aries smiled weakly at her.

"Yeah," he whispered.

"Then just stay awake long enough to get to the ship. Please," Elenora begged.

Doc and Roman supported either side of Aries and helped him limp out of the arena. Elenora looked at Marko.

"Can you go with them and make sure he gets there safely?" she asked him.

"What about you? Aren't you coming with us?" Marko asked. Elenora went to the weapons table and began to put throwing knives into her belt.

"I have one more thing I need to do before I meet back up with you," she said.

Before Marko could protest, she ran off in the direction Nava had gone earlier.

Reji Ex

Meanwhile, in the control room, Vine had a complete visual of the entire prison. She noticed that all the guards were gathered in one location. Her heart sank when she noticed why. She quickly began to re-code the robots' programming. The initial goal was to shut them down, but she noticed Elenora running in. Vine quickly but carefully wrote out codes and was about to enter them into the database.

"Vine?" a voice said. Vine whipped around and glared at the person who spoke.

"Jax," she said coldly.

"What are you doing here?"

"Oh, don't pretend like you care. But we're here to stop your mommy girlfriend," Vine said. Jax sighed and leaned to one side.

"Look, I'm sorry you felt betrayed by me," Jax started but was cut off by Vine scoffing loudly.

"That I felt betrayed? That is some serious gaslighting. You tried to crash us on her prison planet," Vine said.

"Look, I know the truth about what her plan is. She's trying to stop the Milky Way galaxy and the Andromeda galaxy from colliding. This would kill everyone and everything," Jax said.

"She is killing everyone and everything. She's blowing up planets, Jax. How are you okay with that?" Vine pleaded.

"She's not blowing them up. That's ridiculous and not even possible. I mean how can…" his voice trailed off as he looked at the screen. He watched as Elenora plunged a spear into Nava.

"Look at her. She just stabbed her own mother! What's going on with you people?" Jax shouted. Vine took this moment to send the new code, and just like that, the queen's guards were being

The Broken Kingdom of Orion

slaughtered. She smiled at her work. Jax looked at the screen in horror.

"Oh my god! Why did the queen have her robots kill her own army?" she questioned, hoping Jax didn't notice that she launched a code change.

"I...I don't know...I don't understand," Jax muttered.

"Where do you think planets like Helix and Orion are going? What do you think happened to them?" Vine pushed. Jax shook his head.

"No, she didn't lie to me. She had proof that..." his eyes drifted to the screen where Doc and Roman were helping Aries off the post. "He...Queen Nava is a caring mother that had to hide her daughter from a deranged king."

"That defenseless man? The one that's laying half-dead on the ground right now? That's the deranged king? You know Elenora. She wouldn't hurt anyone. What did Nava do to cause such an extreme reaction from her?" Vine questioned.

Jax turned and left the room. Vine watched as Elenora chased after Nava. She saw Nava on a different screen every time. Vine used the loudspeaker to help Elenora as best as she could, but the hallways were winding and confusing. Soon, Elenora and Nava were on a flight of stairs together. Vine watched as Jax also came into view on the cameras. She wished she had sound for the monitors, but all she could do was watch the CCTV footage.

In the stairwell, Elenora threw a knife toward Nava, pinning her long, luxurious sleeve to the wall behind her. Nava tugged at the knife but ended up ripping her sleeve off her dress instead.

"How did you do that?" Nava asked.

Reji Ex

"I was sent to a government military base. I was The General's favorite. You think he wouldn't teach me self-defense in my 21 years of abandonment?" Elenora said snarkily. Jax watched the exchange for the landing just above the staircase the two were on.

"This is all just a big misunderstanding, Ellie. I wanted you to join me," Nava said.

"You shot me, you killed my father, and you blew up my home planet. You abandoned me on Earth and you want me to join you?" Elenora asked.

"Dante is dead?" Nava laughed wickedly. "He's finally dead. I'm finally free!"

"You'll join him soon. Don't worry," Elenora threw another knife toward Nava, hitting her skirt. Nava scoffed and ripped it out.

"This dress was really expensive, Elenora," Nava scolded.

"Why did you do this? Any of this?" Elenora asked.

"You don't know what it's like to be me. I was promised since the day I was born that I would be queen," Nava started.

"You were queen!"

"I was his queen! On his planet, after being his bride. Then a few months later I was his incubator for HIS heir. I was whatever he needed for his kingdom. You know they were highly empathetic on that planet, so they avoided hurting each other's feelings? They spent the entirety of their lives either getting high or giving each other gifts. The job of the king and queen was to keep everyone happy."

"How fucking terrible," Elenora replied sarcastically.

"Yeah, it was. On my planet, the king and queen stomped out the little guy to make sure there was enough food on the table that no one else was invited to. That's the real job of king and queen."

The Broken Kingdom of Orion

"The planet you sent me to had a country where people cut the heads off of royalty like that."

"Oh, I didn't send you there. I was fine having you blow up with everyone else. My stupid, trusted advisor knew about the bomb and kidnapped you. When I found out they were doing lab experiments on you I thought 'good, tying up loose ends,' but he ruined that too by getting rid of the guy. When I got back to Helix, I was shunned. I wasn't their princess anymore. I was Dante's queen, and that didn't sit right with me…so I blew them up too," Nava said.

"That's fine. I'm gonna chop your head off either way," Elenora said, pulling out a knife. Jax had heard enough and stepped forward.

"My queen! I've come to save you," he announced. He stepped between Elenora and Nava. Nava fake gasped and threw herself into Jax's arms to gain his sympathy.

"She was going to kill me! I'm her own mother! Her deranged father turned her against me. She even told me that she killed him," Nava whined as she hugged Jax.

"You bitch!" Elenora roared as she stepped forward. Jax pushed her back and Elenora fell. She tumbled down the steps and lay motionless on the bottom. Jax gasped.

"I didn't mean to do that. I swear, I didn't know she was going to fall back. I just meant to have her step back," Jax explained.

"It doesn't matter. They brought a whole army with them. We're the only two people left on Ceres. We have to escape them while we still can." Nava took Jax's hand and ran up the flight of stairs.

"Wait! I should check on her and make sure she's okay," he said.

"No time! Plus, she's better off dead." With every word that Nava spoke, it became glaringly clear that Jax had chosen the wrong side. He had planned to double-cross Nava. He sincerely didn't mean to push her down the stairs, but the weight of what he did to his friends and how he hurt Elenora by trying to pretend to be on Nava's side, it was too much for him.

Nava quickly led him to a two-person aircraft. To Jax, this was more evidence that she was planning to abandon her own guards when she needed to escape.

"I have to find a doctor. That stupid girl stabbed me," Nava mumbled while she flew out of the atmosphere of Ceres. Jax stayed silent in the seat next to her.

Vine saw the whole thing go down. She saw Jax push Elenora, but she also noticed his hands reach out and try to catch her when he noticed her going backward. That didn't matter. She ran out of the building as fast as she could to get help.

"Marko!" she yelled out as she saw the team loading up in the carrier. Marko turned around and looked at her. "It's Elenora. She's hurt."

Marko didn't waste any time running back into the building. Vine led the way to where Elenora lay at the bottom of the staircase.

"Help me move her into the recovery position," Marko said. The two carefully positioned Elenora so she was laying on her side. Marko assessed the damage. She had a head wound and clearly lost consciousness, but until they could get her to the infirmary, they had no idea if she had a spinal fracture or break.

The Broken Kingdom of Orion

"I don't know what to do. I can't move her, or she could be paralyzed. But we have to go so Aries can get help," Marko said. Over the loudspeaker a delightful ding got the attention of Marko and Vine.

"Attention loyal servants of Queen Nava. You no longer have a use for me. This planet will explode in ten minutes. Please say your goodbyes as there are no more escape pods, Goodbye!" the loudspeaker announced.

"Well, that seems like a sign," Marko said. He quickly scooped up Elenora and ran to the ship. "We have to leave right now!"

"Yeah, Marko, that's the plan," Roman said.

"No! She's blowing up the planet," Vine explained.

"Well, shit. That kind of makes things tough. Buckle up guys, this will not be smooth sailing," Roman said. Vine and Marko strapped Elenora into a seat while she started to gain consciousness.

"Where am I?" she asked.

"Safe…sort of," Marko answered as he strapped himself in his own seat. Elenora looked around before the spacecraft rapidly took off.

"I'm using afterburners for take-off and hyper speed as soon as we're out of the atmosphere. This will cause you to be stuck in your seats until we're a safe distance away," Roman explained. True to his word, the team was unable to move, but as soon as Roman felt that they were a safe distance away the craft evened out.

"What's going on?" Elenora asked.

"Nava-" Marko started but as soon as he said her name the planet behind them exploded. The craft was hit with debris, but other than light shaking, sustained no damages. "Yeah…that."

"We should be home in a few minutes. How's Aries doing, Doc?" Roman asked.

"Lost consciousness but is breathing. So, good so far," Doc said. "How about you, princess? Are you doing alright?"

"I have the worst headache ever, but I'm fine," Elenora said.

"She was pushed down the stairs," Vine said.

"Try not to move until I can check to see if-"

"Broken back. I know," Elenora said.

"There's Juniper," Roman announced. He announced their arrival on the intercom and was granted access onto their ship.

20: Battleship Juniper

The group got Aries and Elenora to the infirmary as soon as they got back to the ship. When Besnik saw Aries he stopped in his tracks.

"What happened back there?" he asked.

"Besnik, you can't let him die. Please, you can't—" Elenora begged before Marko led her away. Doc stood next to Besnik and clapped his hands together.

"Pop quiz, Besnik. Your next patient has deep lacerations on his back and third-degree burns along his abdomen and torso. You're also working against dehydration and the only blood donor for him is also being treated. What do you do first?" Doc asked. Besnik looked at Aries who was still unconscious.

"Lacerations? To stop him from bleeding out," Besnik said.

"How?"

"Clean the wounds and glue them shut instead of sutures. That'll lessen the number of times we'll have to redress the wounds," Besnik answered.

"You get started on that, I'll check up on the princess," Doc said as he started to leave.

"Wait, is that the right answer?" Besnik asked. Doc stopped and looked back at Besnik.

"If he lives then it's the right answer."

"If he dies?" Besnik questioned. Doc put his hand on his protege's shoulder.

"You've been interning for me for over a month now. If I thought you were going to kill our captain I wouldn't leave you alone with him." Doc left without another word and Besnik went to work. He turned Aries onto his side and started cleaning out the deep whip marks that covered his back. He sighed, trying to imagine the cruelty that Aries suffered at the hands of the queen. When he was done he laid Aries back down. He frowned as he noticed blue blood dripping from an odd wound on his neck.

"What is that?" he muttered to himself. He reached out to assess the wound when Aries's unswollen eye snapped open. Aries grabbed Besnik's wrist before he could even touch him. Besnik gasped at the sudden movement but remained calm.

"You're safe, Captain. You're on the Juniper. I was just treating your injuries," Besnik reassured Aries. Aries shook his head. "Can you tell me how you got it?"

"No," Aries said in a harsh whisper.

"Okay, can I at least put a bandage on it?" Besnik asked. Aries nodded.

"Where's my daughter?" Aries asked softly.

"She's being seen by Doc," Besnik said. Aries struggled against the pain to try and get up. Besnik gently held him against the bed. "What are you doing? You're way too injured to be getting up."

"I have to see her," Aries said.

"I can't let you do that. Not before treatment, at least. I'm gonna have to sedate you for—"

"You're not putting me to sleep," Aries cut him off.

"Aries, I need to cut the dead skin away. Do you know how painful that's gonna be? Even with pain killers…"

"I don't care about that. You're not putting me to sleep," Aries said.

"Okay." Besnik pulled up a stool and sat next to Aries. He looked at him at eye level. "Aries, what happened to you?"

"I was tortured."

Besnik shook his head. "You're afraid to sleep. That's a sign of emotional trauma. There's something more, Aries."

"I'm not doing this with you. You're not putting me to sleep," Aries said, looking up at the ceiling.

"Aries—" Besnik started but was cut off by Doc.

"You have to follow the captain's orders. Work around it," he said.

"Elenora?" Aries asked.

"She's fine. She just had a head injury," Doc informed him as he got his equipment ready to treat Aries's burns.

"Nava hurt her?"

"No, I guess it was the Helix boy. She'll live though," Doc said. He injected Aries with a syringe.

"What are you doing?" Aries asked.

"This is really gonna hurt. Last chance to decide you want to be put under," Doc said. Aries shook his head. Doc shrugged and handed Aries a towel. "You're gonna want to bite down on this then."

Aries put the towel in his mouth and gave Doc a thumbs up. Doc began to cut into him. Aries' screams of pain were muffled by the towel, but Besnik needed to help hold him still. When Doc was finished clearing away the burnt, blackened skin, he dressed the wounds. He looked at Besnik.

"Hey, we need saline. You think you can get us a bag?" Besnik nodded and left. When he was out of the room Doc turned to Aries.

"Is there something you're not willing to say to Besnik that you'll tell me?" he asked. Aries sighed and looked up at the ceiling. Doc was his oldest living friend. He was the one that found him after the explosion and brought him to the Juniper.

"Why would she do this to me?" he whispered. He refused to cry. He refused to shed any tears because of that woman. He was determined to overcome her abuse and stay strong. But it was hard. Even treating the wounds hurt him. It's like that was her plan. Either he died by her hand, or he'd still have some torture left before getting better. It was like no matter what he did he could never truly escape her.

"You were good to her, Captain. There's no reason for her to do anything she's done," Doc said. Aries took a shaking breath as he thought about what to say. He knew that Doc probably heard Besnik ask about his mental health, because why else would he send Besnik away just to talk?

"I should have…I should have just taken the chance to escape and live a normal life after Orion. I shouldn't have gone after her," Aries said.

"So why did you?"

"Because she hurt me. Then what did that get me? She just keeps hurting me any chance she gets."

"So why don't you give up then? No one would blame you. Okay, maybe they would because you're some sort of hero figure to them.

The Broken Kingdom of Orion

But, so what. Change your name again and head to Earth," Doc said. He eyed Aries to make sure he got the reaction out of him that he wanted. He could have said any planet but he mentioned Earth on purpose. He knew Aries. He knew what kind of a man he truly was.

"I have to…"

"Have to what?"

"The kids on Eris…" Aries muttered.

"So what? Who cares? They're not your kid. You have your kid. Take her and go," Doc said. Aries was quiet for a second then frowned.

"No. When I was a kid I refused to steal a bird's egg because no parent should have to go through that. No parent should have to go through..." Aries stopped and breathed. He had a sudden realization that he somehow didn't notice before. "No parent should have to go through what I went through. What she put me through. Losing your child is the worst feeling in the universe. I would rather be tortured again than lose Elenora. I have to stop Nava. This isn't even revenge anymore. She won't be allowed to tear any more families apart."

Doc smiled to himself. *"Atta boy,"* he thought.

"I really thought I was going to die back there. I was ready for it. I was okay with it," Aries said.

"And now?"

"I just want to see my daughter. I want to make sure she's okay."

"I've worked for you for twenty years. I've dedicated my life to helping you on your mission. I would never do anything to betray your trust. So trust me when I say you don't want to see her right now," Doc said.

"You told me she was fine, that she just had a head injury. You lied to me?"

Reji Ex

"I did not lie to you. She's just…" Doc groaned. "Okay. I'll go get her."

Doc got up and retrieved Marko and Elenora from another recovery room.

"How are you?" Aries asked Elenora.

"Yes." Elenora smiled. Marko slowly guided Elenora to a chair so she could sit down. He stood by her side and placed a hand on her shoulder.

"El has a head injury and is…acting weird," Marko explained.

"Oh my god, I love that song," Elenora said. Marko looked at his wife, about to say something to her but decided against it. He shook his head and turned his attention to Aries.

"This is fun. You can ask her any question you can think of and will get random trivia instead of an actual answer. Try it," Marko said.

"Okay. What's your favorite color?" Aries asked.

"The USS Barb is the only submarine with a known train sinking in its record," Elenora said. Aries couldn't help but laugh but had to stop because laughing hurt.

"So you think you're gonna live?" Marko asked Aries. Before he could answer Doc chuckled.

"'Course he will. If he listens to doctor's orders. Oh…I guess he won't," Doc joked. Besnik came back with the saline and hooked it up to Aries's IV. Elenora stood up and placed her hand against Aries's face.

"Very bruised," she muttered. Aries sighed.

"Yup. But I'm fine." Aries took her hand in his.

"Your recovery is going to take forever if you don't sleep, you know," Doc said. Aries shook his head. "Well, I can't make you, unless I had a magic syringe that'll put you to sleep if I just poke you here."

Doc injected the medicine into Aries's IV port before he even realized. Aries gasped and pushed him back.

"How could you do that?" he snapped.

"To get you to sleep. I thought that was pretty obvious," Doc said. Aries grabbed Doc by the front of his shirt, but before he could even do anything his vision blurred. Doc caught him by the arm to make sure he didn't fall out of bed and carefully laid him back down.

"Don't fight it, Captain. You're surrounded by people that'll protect you," Doc said. Aries was suddenly unable to keep his eyes open and quickly slipped into a deep sleep.

"What happened to 'work around the captain's orders' Doc?" Besnik asked.

"He'll forgive me. I think. He hasn't executed me yet," Doc answered.

"That's like what Thomas Jefferson said," Elenora said. Marko looked at her suspiciously, not believing she had an actual quote.

"What did he say?" Marko asked.

"Seahawks. 21-10. Hinz was wide receiver. And we got one for the thumb," Elenora confidently replied.

"Wow that was almost a complete thought," Doc said. Besnik shook his head and left the infirmary for the night. He made his way to Roman's room and knocked on the door.

"Can we talk?" he asked when Roman answered. Roman stepped to the side and let him in.

"I wanted to talk to you too, actually," Roman said. Besnik sat on the edge of Roman's bed and looked up at him. "We shouldn't start a relationship."

"Like right now because things are complicated?" Besnik asked.

"No. At all," Roman clarified.

"I don't understand. I thought…I thought we had a connection," Besnik said.

"We did. I mean, we do. And I really enjoyed kissing you," Roman said. He sat next to Besnik and held his hand, causing Besnik to jump up.

"Don't touch me. You're not going to use me if it means nothing to you," he said.

"I didn't say it meant nothing. And I don't want to use you. I just don't think…"

"What?"

"I don't think I'm capable of love. And, I mean, let's be honest. I'm gonna be on the ground at Eris and I don't want to hurt you if…" Roman shrugged. He didn't have to finish the thought for Besnik to know what he meant. Besnik looked away from him.

"You don't think I know that? You're not giving me the chance to speak or decide for myself!" he snapped. Roman stood up and put his hands on Besnik's shoulders. "I said don't touch me."

"Sorry," Roman took his hands off Besnik. "You're right. You should be able to decide your own life. But I…I've never been in love. And you kissed me. You were so sure. It was an amazing kiss, and I've been trying to figure out what it meant."

"It meant that I love you and I thought you felt the same. We've been inseparable since Helix. We had a real connection. I wouldn't have done it if I knew you didn't feel the same way."

"I feel strongly about you. I just don't know what it is, and you deserve someone that's sure about themselves. I just don't want to hurt you. I'm sorry," Roman said.

The Broken Kingdom of Orion

Besnik turned on his heels and left the room. He was on his way back to his own room when he passed Marko and Elenora.

"Woah, strong heartbreak vibes off of you, man," Elenora said. He groaned.

"You can't even tell us your favorite color right now but your empathy is in overdrive?" Besnik snapped.

"I'm sensing a lot of misplaced hostility. Hi, I'm Elenora, your friend. You're not mad at me," she said with a small smile. Besnik sighed.

"You're right. I've just…I've had a long day," Besnik said. Elenora hugged Besnik, which he gladly accepted and hugged her back.

"Remember, the greatest gift is love. If it's real, it'll work. I promise," Elenora said.

"Thanks, Elenora. But I think it's one-sided." She pulled away from him and started walking away.

"That's so weird, Marko," Elenora said.

"What is?" he asked.

"Besnik and Roman give off the same wavelength when they're next to each other. So weird," Elenora rambled before singing softly to herself.

"That's okay, sweetie. Let's get you to bed," Marko said as he led her back to their room.

Aries woke up the next morning and felt something cold covering his face. He panicked, pulled it off, and threw it across the room. He looked around and saw Besnik watching him, horrified.

"That was an ice mask for the swelling on your face," he said.

"Oops," Aries mumbled.

Reji Ex

"It probably needed to be replaced anyways," Besnik replied. Roman brought the ice pack back over to Aries.

"Here Captain, you dropped this…at the back of my head," he said.

"Sorry. Where's Elenora?" Aries asked.

"She's getting treated. It should only take a few minutes."

"I have to go," Aries said, starting to get out of bed.

"Go? Go where? I can't let you leave. You're still injured. You're gonna be in a lot of pain if you try to get up," Besnik said. He gently pushed Aries back onto the bed.

"Fine, can you get me a change of clothes from my cabin, at least?" Aries asked.

"I can do that for you. I'm just waiting on Elenora anyways," Marko piped in. Aries glared at him for a moment.

"Fine. But don't touch anything in there except the closet," Aries instructed. With a mock salute, Marko got up and left the infirmary. He made his way down the long winding hallways of the once cruise liner, turned battleship. He nodded at crewmen and women as he passed them and entered Aries's cabin. He flicked on the light and stopped when he saw the state of the room. The whole room was about as big as a closet. There was only a messy bed, a desk littered with maps and papers, and a small closet. Marko went to the closet and got a change of clothes but stopped when he looked back at the desk again. He knew he shouldn't snoop but he couldn't help himself. He saw maps of the galaxy with x's but Earth was circled. He saw a picture of Aries's wedding day to Nava. Aries was happier in the photo, but he still looked mostly the same. He opened drawers to peek inside. All the drawers held your average desk supplies except the top middle one. That drawer had a pack of cigars, a lighter, and a

The Broken Kingdom of Orion

baby picture. Marko held up the baby picture, noting "Elenora" scribbled on the back. He stared at the baby picture of his wife for a moment before putting it back. He snagged a cigar before making his way back to the infirmary.

Marko placed Aries's clothes on a table next to him, then carefully palmed the cigar to him so Besnik and Doc wouldn't see. Aries slipped it under his pillow.

"You're my favorite son-in-law," Aries said quietly to him.

"Are there others?"

"Not that I know of. Suppose it's possible, though." Aries gently pulled on his IV and decided not to pull it out. He instead cinched the line and grabbed a pair of surgical scissors and cut it.

"What are you doing?" Marko panicked.

"Shut up," Aries ordered. Aries did his best to tie off the IV line.

"That won't hold. Look, just…" Marko started but stopped. He pulled Aries's arm towards him and then safely removed the IV.

"You have medical training?" Aries asked.

"Yes. Well, no. I don't know. I've thought about it," Marko said. Aries started to get dressed before getting out of bed and walking out, bringing the single cigar with him.

"If you want to learn, I can always order Doc to take you on," Aries said.

"Are...Are you okay?" Marko asked as he followed Aries down the hall.

"I'm fine. Not my first assassination attempt. Just the one that was most likely to succeed," Aries said. As they walked down, crewmen stopped and saluted Aries. Most of them looked as if they saw a ghost walking by but held their respect either way. Aries pushed open the doors to the navigation room.

Reji Ex

"Captain on deck," someone announced. Everyone stood at attention, facing Aries. Aries was starting to feel the effects of his injuries as his painkillers wore off. He sat down in his captain's chair while everyone awaited his orders.

"Eris," was all he said. The crew immediately began working to set the location.

"You're not going to be healed enough by the time we get there," Marko said to him. Aries held out his cigar and a crewman lit it without needing to be asked.

"I don't need to be healed. I need a crew that's loyal to me," Aries said. He puffed on his cigar. "Is there anyone here that wouldn't fight for our cause?"

"I'm a computer man, captain, I would be terrible in battle," someone said.

"You're excused from battle. Anyone else?" No one spoke up and Aries gave Marko a smug smile. Marko ignored him and looked out the window at the passing stars. In a different world, Marko would have been upset about Aries using pawn crewmen to fight his battles but given how Aries was currently injured for trading his life for his crew's safety, he figured Aries had a pass. Marko felt something lightly tap his foot. He looked down and frowned at Aries's cigar. Marko looked at Aries and his heart sank as he saw him slumped over the edge of the chair he was in.

"Aries?" he called out. A few crewmembers turned to look at their captain. Marko went over and gently shook him. "Aries!"

Aries was unresponsive.

21: Makemake

Jax and Nava had been on Makemake for a couple of days while she was recovering. During that time, Jax hadn't said much. He often stared out of the window of the palace contemplating the events that happened on Ceres. Aries was dead. Elenora was dead because he killed her. Nava made all sorts of confessions that she didn't even know Jax heard. Jax's head was spinning. He was told for years one thing, and in one day the entire illusion crashed around him. He spent years being friends with them and he crashed their ship on Ceres because of lies he was told about one man. His heart hurt at the pain he had caused. And worse, on the day they arrived Jax noticed dried blue blood under Nava's nails as he helped her out of the craft to get to a doctor. He had no doubt that she was at fault for Aries's injuries.

He felt disgusted with himself. He'd caused two deaths by trusting the wrong person. His friend, who he was sent to help protect, was dead because of him. He didn't mean to push her down the stairs. He only meant to push her back. But Nava was quick to tell him that it didn't matter, that her own daughter was better off dead. Why send him to protect her if Nava felt that way about her? What was she trying to do with him? What was her game?

He was being eaten alive by his guilt. He was done being a pawn. He had nothing left to lose, so he went over to her lavish bed where she was resting and asked her outright.

"Why did you send me to Earth?"

Nava lifted her sleep mask to glare at who was talking to her. She put her sleep mask back on and laid her head back. "I've told you why, Jax," she replied.

"You said it was to protect Elenora from Aries," Jax said.

"Yes."

"Then why did you say she was better off dead." Nava sighed and clapped her hands. A robot brought in a drink for her. She sat up and grabbed the drink. The robot bowed and left. She took the sleep mask off and sipped from her straw while looking at Jax. Jax could tell she was thinking. He caught her in a lie, and she didn't have another in place for when she got called out.

"Jax, you're not a parent. You wouldn't understand. Elenora was too…too poisoned by Aries, and it was your fault," she said finally. Jax scoffed.

"You said it was Elenora who killed him," he pointed out.

Nava gasped. "I said no such thing!"

"You did. You said she killed Aries. She called you a bitch and charged you and that's when I stepped in," Jax recalled. Nava nodded slowly.

"Yes, before you killed her. You're remembering wrong, Jax. It happens when you do something horrible. Your brain plays tricks to protect itself. You only remember me saying that, probably for your brain to justify why killing her was okay. But you remembered that she attacked me and stabbed me. That's something you remember clearly. Right?" the Queen said.

The Broken Kingdom of Orion

"I didn't mean to push her down the stairs," Jax said.

"Of course, Jax. No one means to hurt anyone," Nava dropped her drink on the ground and laid back in her bed. A robot immediately came into the room and started cleaning up her discarded drink.

"Except you when you beat Aries to death?" Jax asked. Nava's eyes snapped open and she glared at Jax.

"I had to protect myself from him. He is a monster!" she yelled.

"Why? Because you said he was?"

"Yes! And I am your queen! You don't have to believe anything unless I tell you to. And I demand that you drop this at once!" she screeched. Jax stared down at the ground at his feet as if it was about to shift and the world was going to swallow him. He was devastated. Everyone was right, but he grew up listening to Nava. He had no choice but to believe her this whole time. And it had cost him everything.

"Is it true that you blew up Orion?" Jax asked slowly. Nava blinked away her anger before answering.

"Yeah? So what? It wasn't a planet that worshiped me. They worshiped him," Nava said. Jax nodded and turned around. He walked away. He left the palace and wandered around in the streets. He hadn't thought blowing up a planet was possible. Since Nava confessed, then it was to be believed that she also blew up Helix. He was never going home. He pushed away the woman that he loved for the hope of returning to Helix, something long gone. He was the only one from Helix. Nava told him he was the only one because Helix was safe and he was going on a secret mission for her.

Everyone he ever knew and loved from his home was dead.

Jax fell to his knees right in the middle of the street at the thought. He hid his face in his hands in agony over what he'd done. Then he

Reji Ex

slowly looked up as a realization hit him. He was in the middle of the street, but no one was around him. There were no vehicles, no people, no pets. Nothing. The street was empty. He got up and went straight back to the castle. He pushed the bots out of his way to get to the queen's room. She groaned when she saw him enter.

"What now, Jax?" she asked.

"I just was on a walk and noticed that…there's no people here." Jax tried to keep his voice even as if he was just asking and not accusing her of something.

"Yes, I couldn't let them have babies after I took the kids to Earth. This planet wasn't safe with the war going on and all," Nava said.

"You're preventing childbirth? How?" he asked.

"I had the ladies put drugs in the food. I couldn't let them know or else they'd go on food strike, obviously," Nava explained.

"And the ladies are?"

"The robots, of course. Humans are so fragile. They die so easily. Not only that but the ungrateful people of Eris are uprising. I just gave them their children back too," Nava said. Jax looked around the room. Everything was red and gold. He wondered if it was supposed to be blood red. He wondered if it was symbolic for the blood on her hands or if she just chose it as her motivation.

"Nava, what did Aries do?" Jax asked.

"What?"

"You blew up Orion and hunted him down, hid his daughter from him. What did he do to deserve this?" Jax asked. Nava growled.

"Get out!" she yelled. She picked up a hairbrush from her side table and whipped it at Jax. He ducked out of the way. "It is not your job to question me! You are supposed to worship me!" she yelled.

The Broken Kingdom of Orion

"I can't even ask without you blowing up? What are you hiding?" Jax asked.

"Guards! Guards! I want him dead!" she yelled. Robots had entered the room and turned their eyes to Jax. He ran to the terrace as they closed in on him.

"I want him dead!" Nava yelled again. Jax quickly started to climb down from the balcony. He lost his footing and fell back. He landed hard on the ground but didn't have the chance to catch his breath before needing to run away from the robots chasing him. He ran as fast as he could, changing directions whenever a robot appeared, until he was cornered in the ship hangar.

"Stop! You are being arrested for crimes against the queen," the robots said in unison. In a panic, Jax climbed into the first spacecraft he could get to. He locked the doors behind him and covered his head in panic. He hyperventilated while the robots rocked the ship. He was a terrible pilot and hardly knew how to even start the thing. He really wished Vine was there. He knew she'd at least be able to access the system and get the thing in the air. He had no choice but to attempt something or the robots would kill him. He crawled to the cockpit and fumbled with buttons. He got the craft to light up and the engine roared to life. The robots instinctively backed off when the spacecraft started. Jax pushed more buttons and the craft started to elevate.

The ship bumped around the hangar before Jax pulled up on the handles. The ship crashed through the ceiling of the hangar and Jax was flying free. He panicked and pulled on the handles trying to get the craft to do something other than fly around randomly. Eventually, he successfully broke through the atmosphere of the planet. When he was outside the pull of gravity he let go and let the ship float freely. He sighed in relief, but he was far from relaxed.

Reji Ex

He was no longer under the immediate threat of death but other uncertain death awaited him. He checked the gage thingy and the other gage thingy and quickly realized he had no idea what he was doing. He didn't even know how to land. There had to be a manual somewhere. He started opening drawers and compartments looking for it. A red light started blinking and Jax looked at it. The button said "incoming call" so he pushed it.

"What do you think you're doing, Jax?" Nava said over the speaker.

"What are you doing?" he parrotted, "You were gonna have me killed for asking why you hated Aries so much? How is that helping your case?" He could feel the tears of fear pricking at his eyes. He was thankful that the phone was a speaker system and not a hologram so Nava couldn't see him cry.

"You have no right to question me. Aries deserved his death! Elenora was half Aries, so she deserved her death too!" Nava shouted.

"WHY?" Jax shouted back. Nava paused. Her heavy breathing was still heard over the phone or else Jax would have thought she hung up on him.

"You can't fly your ship. You have no home planet to go to. You have no friends anymore. You have nowhere to go. Why don't you just kill yourself while you're alone up there? There's nothing left for you," Nava said in an eerily calm voice.

"Alright, fine. If death is the only thing I have left then you should be able to tell me why you had so much hatred for him. I heard what you said to Elenora about never having your own life, but I'm not buying that. You could have just killed him and made the whole planet suffer," Jax said.

"No, Orions are empaths. I would feel their pain if I did that."

"Then…why? Why all of this?" Jax asked. His voice was small, and he worried that she didn't even hear him at first but then she answered.

"I was sold to Aries. Then when I came home expecting my old life back, I was berated by my parents. They believed Aries owned me. And when I told them that I killed him when I blew up the planet…they said that my planet was gone, and I failed as their queen. So I killed them too. Blew up the whole place," Nava explained.

"But that was your parents. Not Aries," Jax said.

"Ugh, Aries. I hated that name. His name is Dante. But it doesn't matter. He's nothing now. I beat him to a bloody pulp and shot whatever was left. There's no way he survived. But he deserved it. He survived the explosion. Tried to get revenge for it."

"So you're mad that he survived you?"

"And I've been looking for the perfect planet ever since. One that would worship me. And if they didn't then…boom."

"Like Helix…and me."

"Exactly. Go ahead and run, Jax. There's nothing that can save you now. All the bots on my network know who you are. There's not a planet that you can go to that won't get you killed," Nava said. The light went out and he knew she had ended the call.

She was right, there was nothing he could do. There was nowhere he could go. He burnt the bridges on Juniper. He could beg for Vine's forgiveness, but he was so ashamed of what he did. He had screamed at her and tried to hurt her. He really was unhinged from working for Nava.

Reji Ex

He stared at the random buttons and switches and sighed. He was floating to nowhere, and soon, he was gonna run out of air unless he found a place to land. Not only that but he had no clue how to land. Everything in his life was a disaster and Nava was right, he should just end it all. He sat on the ground and looked around. There wasn't even anything to end his life within the spacecraft. He couldn't find anything useful.

There were no weapons. He found some dehydrated food and water. He couldn't find anything to fight off robots or commit suicide with.

He did, however, find the manual. He read through it and figured out the controls. Now he just needed to have a game plan. Earth was an option, but the people of Earth were not as welcoming as they thought they were. He would have to quarantine for a week until they decided he didn't have any space germs, then he'd have to live on 51 forever.

Jax was full of regret. Elenora was dead by his hands and the last thing they talked about was…wait. He quickly jumped into the cockpit and pushed the buttons that the manual told him to push. He was very shaky while flying but he had plenty of time to figure out the controls while he was trying to get where he was going.

He had no hope of redemption with Vine. He knew this. Everything they once had was over for good, and he never expected her to forgive him. He was awful. He had no real reason to lay his hands on her. He doesn't even know why he acted so violently against her. Maybe the queen drugged him or something. Maybe he was just acting out in fear because of the queen's lies. He had no idea why any of this was happening, but he knew there was something he could do to save his soul.

The Broken Kingdom of Orion

He remembered that Juniper was headed to Eris. He had some friends on Eris. He just needed to get there and possibly help the crew of Juniper. He didn't know how well this was going to work out for him. Those robots were on Eris, and they all knew who he was and would target him. Maybe he could use that in his favor during the battle. Maybe he could do anything at all to be on the good side for once before he's ultimately killed.

Jax fumbled around with control buttons and switches until he got the ship to do what he wanted. He typed into the navigation system at least ten times before it understood that he was trying to get to Eris. Once navigation was up, he just needed to fly the course of the red line on the screen, and boom, everything was working. He munched idly at the food that was on the ship while he read the manual some more. He was beginning to relax from the trauma he'd just endured. Truthfully, it made him more depressed about his treatment toward Vine. He missed her. He wanted her to hold him and tell him everything was going to be okay. He wished there was something he could do to make it up to her, but he knew deep down that it was over. Everything was over for him. The last thing he could possibly do was go to Eris and help fight for the right side this time and die on the good guy's team. He wanted redemption before his death.

Reji Ex

22: Battleship Juniper

When Aries woke, the first thing he realized was that he wasn't in pain anymore. Besnik was standing over him, and Elenora was sitting beside him. He smiled at his daughter and then realized Besnik had just pulled a syringe out of his IV. Besnik was somber and not his normal, nervous self. He seemed stoic like he finally discovered his purpose and he was no longer the spineless follower that he was when he first joined Aries's team. Aries looked at him with confusion as he discarded the needle that he pulled out of Aries's IV.

"What did you just do?" Aries asked.

"I just woke you up from your medically induced coma. You've been out for about a week," Besnik answered.

"What? You can't do that!" Aries yelled. Aries sat up suddenly but the stabbing headache that came with the movement caused him to clutch his head and lay back down.

"Well, you were unconscious at the time. Doc and I wanted to restrain you, but Elenora voted against that and she had medical power over you since she's your next of kin," Besnik explained, completely unconcerned about his headache.

The Broken Kingdom of Orion

"That's mutiny!" Aries growled through gritted teeth.

"You flat-lined, Aries! You died, and we brought you back! What were we supposed to do? Let you do it again?" Besnik shouted back.

"Besnik, you are out of line," Aries said.

"I'm out of line for saving you from yourself? Do you want me to just let you die next time you decide to walk out of the infirmary?"

"I expect you not to put me in a medical coma."

"Look at your daughter and tell her that. It was her choice because of your decision to leave."

"I needed to get the crew to Eris," Aries said.

Besnik slammed his clipboard onto the table beside him in frustration. "Someone else could have sent your orders in. It didn't have to be you."

"Yes, it did!"

"Why?"

"Because I don't want them to see me as weak!" Aries snapped. Besnik gave Aries a confused look and shook his head. Besnik's boiling blood began to calm down and he was suddenly no longer interested in winning this screaming match. He became more concerned about the mental health of his patient.

"No one thinks you're weak, Captain. They all see you as the man brave enough to risk his life for his crew. The man who was sentenced to death and walked away from it," Besnik said. Aries fiddled with the bite scar on the side of his neck. The mark that he did not permit Besnik to see. When Aries was unconscious, Besnik was able to clean the wound without Aries knowing. He noticed that it was a perfect bite but didn't think anything more of it. Aries was beaten, so of course, she would bite him. Besnik knew what happened now. He couldn't say it, it was something Aries would have to admit to when he was feeling comfortable and safe enough to do so. But that vicious bite on Aries's neck told Besnik exactly what kind of hell that damn queen put him through.

"I know how rumors spread," Aries said quietly. Elenora realized what he was talking about.

"Oh. Dad, I didn't tell anyone what happened," she said. Aries looked at her, then rolled over onto his side to face away from her.

"No one knows?" he asked.

"Knows what?" Besnik asked as if he didn't know the answer. Aries and Elenora stayed silent. Elenora knew it wasn't her secret to tell. "Aries, if you're injured then I have to know."

"She didn't do anything to me," Aries responded quickly. Besnik sat down next to Aries, facing him.

"Some injuries aren't physical, they're mental. Both injuries need to heal," Besnik said. Aries rolled to his other side so he was facing Elenora instead of Besnik.

"I don't want to talk about it. I'm fine. She didn't hurt me," Aries said.

"Dad—"

Aries cut off Elenora. "Are we close to Eris?"

"We are expected to be there tonight," Besnik said.

"Am I cleared to leave the infirmary?" Aries asked. Besnik nodded and removed Aries's IV port. Aries started to get out of bed.

"You don't have to fight with us. We understand," Elenora said.

"No, this is my battle. I'm gonna finish it," Aries replied. Besnik handed Aries a change of clothes and Elenora left him to get dressed. She went to her room where she met up with Marko.

"How's your dad?" he asked. Elenora shrugged and plopped down onto the bed.

The Broken Kingdom of Orion

"Stubborn. He's healed pretty quickly though. Thanks again for…you know… CPR until Besnik and Doc got there," she said.

"Hey, it's what any son-in-law of a formally famous king turned space pirate would do. Our lives aren't abnormal at all," he joked. Elenora chuckled. She looked out the bedroom window in thought. Marko lay next to her and pulled her close to his chest.

"What's going through your pretty head?" he asked softly.

"I'm keeping a secret for Aries and it's eating him. If he just talked about it then he could start getting help, I think. But, like I said, he's stubborn and won't tell anyone."

"How do you know this secret if he won't tell anyone?"

"The queen told me. Probably to humiliate him," Elenora said. She snuggled into her husband for comfort.

"Well, that's part of the problem. He had no control of who found out and when. Now he does. He won't say it because then he loses that control that Nava took from him," he said. Elenora hadn't thought of it like that. She sighed at the thought of all the trauma that the queen caused for Aries specifically.

"I just wish I could help him," she said.

"What exactly is the secret? I promise it will stay with just me, but you seem like you need to talk about it so it's not bringing you down, too," Marko said. Elenora sat up and looked at him. Marko did the same. She took a couple of cleansing breaths, trying to clear her head to come up with the right words to tell him.

"The queen made a deal with him. She told him that she wouldn't harm me if… if she used him, physically," Elenora said, carefully.

"Oh," was the only thing that Marko could come up with to say. Elenora looked at him, expecting something more. Truthfully, Marko didn't have anything more to say. He knew what she meant to say but he didn't know how to handle this sort of thing.

"I wish I knew how to help you. And him. But I can't do anything more than be your support person," he said. He hated seeing his wife feeling so hopeless. He hated seeing Aries hurt so badly. He hated that the galaxy was so fucked up because of one person. Elenora and Marko cuddled for a peaceful moment before a tone went over the loudspeaker.

"Attention, crew members. We are nearing our destination of Eris. If you will be engaging in battle, please make your way to the artillery. Otherwise, please man your station. Thank you," the person on the speaker said. Elenora and Marko sighed and got out of bed. They silently walked to the artillery to arm up before landing on Eris. Aries met up with them at the artillery room. He looked at Elenora and shook his head.

"No," he simply said.

"What do you mean 'No'?"

"You're staying here," Aries said firmly.

"Look, your crew isn't military. They're just ragtag fighters, no offense. I actually have military training. I was raised on a military base. I'm proficient in weapons and bomb defusing. You need me," Elenora said. Aries shook his head. "Well, you actually can't stop me. I can be just as stubborn as you."

Aries groaned in frustration when he realized she was right. She was the one person on this ship that he truly had no control over, and she knew it. He wasn't going to stop her from joining the crew on the ground.

"I want you to wear a vest at least," he told Elenora. He grabbed one of the protective vests off of a rack and handed it to her.

The Broken Kingdom of Orion

"If not everyone gets a vest—"

"Oh, they will, not everyone chooses to wear it. Some sort of god complex. Feeling invincible or something. But you have to listen to me because I'm your father." Elenora smiled and gave a fake salute.

"Yes, Captain," she said. Aries hugged Elenora tightly.

"Whatever happens today, I'm not losing you again," he said to her. She hugged him back.

"We'll be fine," Elenora told him. Aries walked away to start giving battle orders to the rest of the crew. There were people who went into battle, people who flew planes, and people that stayed behind to man the Juniper while everyone was doing their respective missions. There weren't that many people to actually fight a whole planet-sized war and everyone knew that. This didn't stop them from trying to liberate this planet from tyrants.

The crew landed on Eris, and immediately, they were met with gunshots. The crew knew what to do. They weren't a regulated military by any means but some of them spent a good chunk of their lives training for this. They found cover and returned fire. Elenora and Marko and Aries were behind a building.

"There are too many of these robot things!" someone shouted. Aries peeked around the corner and shot at the robots. He emptied his magazine and sat back against the building to reload.

"We're gonna run out of rounds. There are too many of them and not enough of us. We can empty mags as much as we want but we're still outnumbered," he said.

"I think I have an idea," Elenora said. She pulled her necklace out of her shirt and pushed the diamond into the pendant.

"Your necklace from The General?" Aries questioned.

"What is your situation?" the pendant asked.

Reji Ex

"Umm...we're on Eris and under attack by an army of robots," Elenora replied.

"They're back on Earth. They'll never make it in time," Aries said. As soon as the words of doubt left his mouth, a portal opened up and an army of Earth people poured out, followed by The General.

"General!" Elenora said. The General saluted Elenora who saluted back.

"We were just testing a portal machine from scientists in Sweden when we got your signal. You got lucky."

"I don't believe it," Aries said in awe. The General smirked at him.

"Believe it, Captain. Now, how can we be of service," The General asked. A robot came around the corner and aimed its gun, but upon seeing Elenora, lowered it.

"Princess located," the robot said.

Aries shot the robot and twisted off its head. "Here, anyone that looks like this needs to be shot," he said, handing the head to The General. Aries looked at Elenora for a second.

"What?" she questioned.

"The robots are programmed to not shoot you," Aries said. Elenora nodded, understanding what Aries wasn't saying. Nava kept her end of the deal.

"Okay, well, you heard him, men. Shoot anyone that looks like this discarded head," The General ordered, holding up the robot's head. The army left with a "sir, yes, sir" and suddenly the teams were even.

Aries fought alongside Elenora. Marko hung back to help the people who got injured. Anytime a bot spotted Elenora, they lowered their weapons.

"We have to get past the bots," Aries told Elenora.

"There's no way we can safely do that," she replied.

"You can. You're not their target. They have orders not to harm you."

"Why do we even need to get past them? The battle's here."

"The civilians. We have to find them. Keep them safe. They have to be hidden somewhere," Aries said.

"What do we do then?" Elenora asked.

"Follow me, stay close," he ordered.

"You are not running straight into a firing zone," Elenora said. Aries took off running towards the closest building, barely escaping gunshots. Elenora, on the other hand, was not targeted at all. They ducked into an empty building and weren't pursued by the bots. Aries checked the house while Elenora watched the door.

"There's no one here," Aries said.

"Now where?"

"The next building I want to check out is immediately next door. Bots to the left, building on the right. Follow me," Aries said. The two ran out of the building and into the next. No people were in that one either. This continued until they finally reached the old school. Aries went into the basement just to check, and there he found the people of Eris huddled in masses, protecting each other from the noises above. The room was dark and only when Aries opened the door, was light shed on the people.

He stared into the dark room. He didn't feel their anger or fear. He felt…something he couldn't quite understand. The people cowered more as Aries opened the door further. They didn't know who he was and didn't know if he was there to finish them off. They've had one hell of a week trying to survive the mass shootings put on by the queen's robots. It was as if she was planning a genocide because they started an uprising. Like she was tired of trying to win them over, so she was going to kill them and move on.

"I'm Aries. I'm here to help you," Aries announced. Elenora followed Aries down the stairs. She was horrified upon seeing the conditions that these people were living in while trying to hide from the queen. She'd obviously heard similar stories from Earth, but witnessing it firsthand was something truly horrendous. She thought the days of genocide were over, that no one truly that evil would ever live again. But as she saw what was happening around her she realized evil was inevitable and repetitive. Thankfully, she knew it never succeeded. People like her and Aries and their whole crew were there to stop it.

"El, go back to the front line. Tell them to protect this building. And, hey, listen to me. They won't shoot you, so don't be afraid to run right through the firefight. I would never tell you to put yourself in harm's way, but you need to hurry" he instructed. Elenora said nothing and quickly ran out of the building.

"I have a whole army fighting to free you," Aries said.

"Why should we believe you? How do we know you're not working for the queen?" a girl said. She stood up and walked right up to Aries. She was his daughter's age. If the queen organized the whole trip to Earth thing, then this girl had probably been at Area 51 with Elenora.

"What's your name?" Aries asked. The girl stood up straight with confidence against Aries. He respected that.

"My name is Kayo."

"Okay, Kayo. You went to Earth. Right? I brought The General and his army to help me fight for your planet. Is that enough reason to trust me?" Aries asked. Kayo looked back at a young man who was obviously her lover based on the emotions she was giving off when she looked at him. The man nodded at her, and Kayo looked back at Aries.

"Okay, fine. Sure. We trust that you're here to save us. But who died and left you in charge?" Kayo said with an attitude. Aries thought for a second.

"Well, my father did technically, but he left my planet to get medical treatment. It's possible he's actually still alive," Aries said. Kayo blinked in surprise, not really expecting a true answer from him.

"In a few hours, I expect this battle to be over one way or another. Does anyone here have a gun or a weapon and is willing to fight?" Aries asked. A few proud Erisians raised their hands.

"Great, we'll need the manpower. The rest of you stay here until it's safe. You'll know because there won't be any more gunshots," Aries said. He left the basement with the others who were willing to fight and went back into the fray.

23: Eris

Elenora took a terrifying step out of the schoolhouse and into the light of day. The battle in the distance was loud, and she was instructed to run right through it. She was trembling with fear, but Aries had assured her that the robots wouldn't shoot her. The army was informed of who to take out, and no robot had vibrant blue hair like she did. She'd be noticed right away by Aries's crew and the army. No one would aim for her. *Oh dear god*, what if a stray bullet caught her and she got hurt or worse? But, she trusted Aries. He'd promised her she'd be safe.

The quickest way to get to the other side was straight through the middle. She took a deep breath to steady herself, then ran. The battle didn't stop but it seemed like she was surrounded by a protective bubble. Wherever she was running, the bullets avoided. She successfully crossed the battlefield and dove behind the structure where Vine, Roman, Marko, and The General were.

"What the hell was that? What were you thinking?" The General scolded. Elenora took a second to catch her breath then nervously laughed out her fears.

The Broken Kingdom of Orion

"I-I don't know. Aries told me to do it," she said with a slight tremor in her voice.

"You could have gotten yourself killed. If Aries told you to jump off a bridge, would you?" he yelled. Elenora thought for a second and nodded.

"I trust him with my life, General. He told me I wouldn't get hurt and I didn't," she said. The General's glare at her softened. Elenora told The General about the school and the civilians inside, and they got the army to shift location to better protect the school building. They caught up with Aries and the new recruits.

"Glad to see you came back, Captain," The General said.

"You didn't think I came to fight?" Aries challenged.

"Oh no, I didn't think you'd survive," The General teased.

"I've survived a lot since the last time I saw you," Aries said.

"Yeah! We killed him and he woke up the next day," Roman said.

"Killed?"

"I was not dead. I only flatlined," Aries corrected. Before The General could even question what he meant, Aries sprung to action, guns drawn. He shot, dodged bullets, and jumped over obstacles to get to the other side. He pulled out his jack-knife, stabbing and slashing at bots. He was his own personal army.

"Hey, it just occurred to me, but how did a little prince grow up to be a killing machine?" Roman asked his brother, who just shrugged in response.

"Sorry, did you say prince?" The General asked.

"Oh yeah. Aries was the king of a planet," Marko explained. The General was too surprised to speak. *King of a whole planet?* There were people on Earth that were willing to kill to have that kind of power. The General joined Aries, shooting, dodging, and rolling out of the way of attacks. He followed Aries to the other side.

"They don't serve our queen!" robots said in unison when laying eyes on them.

"I feel like I just fell straight into a horror movie," The General said.

"Yup. If I knew she was this much of a creep I would have never married her," Aries grumbled. He jumped to action. The General followed suit.

"Did you say you married her? The person who did this was your wife?" Aries was caught off guard and turned to face The General. He turned his back to a bot and got shot in the back. The General returned fire and killed the bot. He dragged Aries to cover.

"Are you hurt?" Aries ripped his scorched shirt off and threw it on the ground as it burnt up.

"Damn it, those stupid plasma balls. They burn and hurt when they hit you but that's it," Aries stood up and brushed himself off. The General was able to see the burn scars that blotched the majority of Aries's chest.

"What happened to you?"

"This isn't the time to get to know one another. We have to go back out there," Aries said. The General took his jacket off and handed it to Aries to cover up.

"No, we have a second. Sit down. You were just hit with a...did you call it a plasma ball? That had to have hurt at least a little. Take a second," The General urged. Aries hesitated for a moment but sat down. The General stood ready to shoot if a bot tried to bother them.

"I hope you know, you got what I always wanted," Aries said.

"And what's that?"

The Broken Kingdom of Orion

"Elenora. She is everything to me and I missed the first 20 years of her life. It hurts. We hardly connect. I mean, we're both putting effort in and it's gonna take time, but that was something I wouldn't even have to worry about if she wasn't stolen from me."

"Hey, I did not take her. But you're right, you were cheated out of being her father. But you have this chance now. She clearly cares about you and trusts you. She ran right through the battlefront, and when I asked her why, she said it was because you told her to," The General replied.

"She beat the shit out of someone on my ship who was trying to mess with her. And she is pretty proficient with weapons. You taught her that?"

"I didn't ever have kids of my own, so I thought boot camp was a good alternative for kindergarten," The General joked. Aries chuckled.

"She's too sweet and innocent for this. For anything I have to offer. She's a princess. She deserves better than battle fronts and liberating planets," Aries said.

"Look, Earth is more of a mess than you think. Just because the queen isn't involved with Earth doesn't mean it doesn't have its own problems."

"As a father, you want what's best for your kids. I could have never raised Elenora after Orion blew up," Aries said.

"But now she's found a home with you."

"I know you love her, and you'll give her a safe life," Aries said.

"But she's yours, Captain. I can't take your kid from you again. Think of it this way, years of living with me on the military base made her ready for the life you have to offer her. Don't push her away because you think she deserves better. I can tell where this conversation is headed and if you're gonna ask me, the answer is no. I'm not gonna take Elenora. Her options are you or staying on this planet." Aries was about to say something when he noticed movement in the distance.

"Wait...Did you see that? That looked like—" Aries was cut off by Elenora running up to him and hugging him.

"Dad, are you alright?" she asked.

"Me? I'm fine. You're worried about me?" Aries questioned.

"Uh, yeah. You just got out of the infirmary. You shouldn't even be here and now you're getting hurt again," Elenora ranted. Aries put a hand on her shoulder to calm her down.

"Hey. I'm fine," he said calmly.

"Wait, those scars just happened to you?" The General questioned. Aries ignored him and stood up. He looked back at where he saw the person running.

"This might sound crazy, but I think I saw Jax running that way," he said.

"Jax?" Vine questioned.

"If he's here then that means she's here," Elenora said bitterly.

Aries, Elenora, and Vine followed the direction that Aries saw Jax. The direction led to a cave.

"We're not really going in there. Right?" Vine asked.

"If that's where Jax is, then we have to," Elenora said. She took off down the cave. Aries followed after her, followed by Vine. The cave had its own lighting system that was turned on. The group had no issue seeing what was ahead of them. The cave turned into some sort of underground building. It was no longer rocks and dirt but was suddenly metal. Footprints echoed from down the hall and the group followed after them. The hall led to a great big opening. In the middle of the opening was a massive machine connected to a series of computers.

"What is that?" Vine asked.

"It's…it's a bomb. She's gonna blow up the planet," Aries said.

"Okay, let's get started, Vine," Elenora prompted. Vine and Elenora approached the bomb. Vine took to the computers as Elenora began trying to take off a panel on the side.

"What are you doing?" Aries asked semi-horrified.

"This bomb is clearly controlled by the computers or else it wouldn't be attached to them. Computers are my specialty, thanks to you," Vine said.

"And I've been taking classes on bomb defusing since I was seven. I need your knife to get this metal panel off," Elenora added. Aries complied and tossed his knife to his daughter.

"I'll take out the trigger coding so no one here or outside the planet can activate the bomb," Vine said.

"And I'm dismantling the wiring so, regardless, the bomb can't go off," Elenora explained. Aries watched the girls work and felt fatherly pride at how brilliant his daughter was. Vine suddenly looked back at Aries unexpectedly. Aries looked behind him and saw Jax standing there, watching in awe.

"You're still alive?" Jax sputtered.

"Aries, kill him, please?" Vine requested. Aries got his gun out and Jax took off down the tunnel. Aries followed him. Jax ran down a corridor that led to a dead end. He turned to face Aries who was pursuing him.

"I didn't know you survived," Jax said.

"That's not a valid argument for betraying us." Aries backhanded Jax with his pistol, and Jax fell backward. He felt the blood pouring out of his split lip and scrambled to put distance between himself and Aries.

"Wait, please. Let me explain," Jax pleaded.

"You know, Jax. You betrayed my hospitality, crashed my ship, got my loyal crew captured. Of course, me trading my life for theirs was entirely my decision, but you were planning on my capture. You had me tortured, whipped, beaten, raped, sentenced to death. Fine. All of that is forgivable. But you did one thing that I can't ever forgive." Jax had backed himself entirely against the wall as Aries ranted. He was trapped, and there was nowhere he could run. He was finally going to die.

"You hurt my daughter, and that's inexcusable," Aries said slowly. He raised his pistol to Jax's head. For a split second, Jax was filled it terror, but his terror quickly dispersed and he bowed his head in acceptance.

"What are you doing?" Aries asked. Jax didn't say anything. He just bowed before Aries and accepted his death. "Any, umm...Any last words?"

"No. I deserve this," Jax answered quietly. Aries was going to pull the trigger. He had planned to end Jax's life. He was capable of killing. But something inside him twisted. He thought about his daughter and how he promised her he was going to be a better man. He groaned at his internal dilemma and put his pistol back in the holster.

"You're under arrest then," Aries decided. Jax looked up at him.

"What?"

"Yeah, you're under arrest for treason. There's a jail on the ship that you'll be living in for a while," Aries said as he jerked Jax up and led him away. Aries led them back to the girls working on disarming the bomb.

"Is this disarmed yet?" he asked. Vine looked up.

"Why is he still alive?" she asked.

"Because he's being arrested."

"But-"

"I'm Captain. I get the final say," Aries said. Vine pouted and faced the computer again. She tapped away at the computer.

"I can't break past the firewall. El, are you having better luck?" Vine asked.

"Yup. It's no IED but the wiring is relatively the same. Only issue is there's multiple trigger points and I have to keep going around. This is a massive bomb," Elenora said from the other side of the bomb.

"Vine, is it password protected?" Jax asked.

Vine glared at him. "Yes," she snapped.

"Try 'Dante'," Jax suggested. Vine typed the name into the password and was granted access.

"Unbelievable. She's completely psycho," Vine ranted.

"Agreed," Aries said. Vine did more typing and then the computer beeped.

"I think the trigger is disabled. Elenora?"

"Last wire was cut on my end," Elenora said.

"Now what?" Aries asked.

"Someone needs to carefully dismantle everything piece by piece," Elenora said.

"That shouldn't be too hard. The army is here. They should know how to do it," Vine said. Elenora handed Aries's knife back to him.

"The bomb will not go off. The rest is up to someone else though."

Aries shook his head. "You two just defused a planet-destroying bomb and you're acting like it was no big deal," Aries said. Elenora shrugged.

"Hey, it was either gonna work or it was no longer our problem. Besides, like I said, I was trained for this. Not exactly on this grand scale, but, yeah." The group walked back out of the cave.

"What took you so long?" The General asked.

"There's a bomb down there. Elenora and Vine disabled it, but they told me your men can dismantle the thing. It's supposed to blow up the planet," Aries said. The General's eyes widened but he cleared his throat.

"Yes, we'll get someone on that. The battle's dying down. Those bots were really easy to take down. The person who made them wasn't exactly expecting a coup d'état."

Aries shrugged. He took out his gun and checked the magazine.

"I'm out of bullets," Aries said. Elenora offered him another mag. "I can't take this from you."

"It's almost over. You need enough to get back to safety and then you can reload," Elenora instructed. The group made their way back to their crew.

"This man goes to the brig. If anyone is free to follow Vine to a cave, there's a bomb that needs to be taken apart," Aries ordered. A few soldiers and crewmen followed Vine back over enemy lines while a couple took Jax back to a cruiser and headed for the ship. Aries looked around and assessed the situation. The bots were submitting. There were only a few hundred left and they were quickly being taken out. The battle was over. Only a few bots still stood. The people of Eris were safe.

"Roman! It is an honor to serve the queen," one bot suddenly called out.

Aries gasped. He knew that phrase. Aries aimed his gun at the bot and killed it, but it was too late. The mind control was already in Roman's veins, and there was nothing anyone could do to stop it. Roman grabbed Aries's hair and pulled back, settling a knife to his throat. The army aimed their guns at Roman.

"No! Don't shoot him," Aries said. He heard Roman breathing heavily like he was struggling to fight against the mind control. Before, Aries wouldn't hesitate to just kill the would-be assassin, but this was Roman. He didn't have a choice but to protect his friend.

"Roman? Are you still with me?" Aries asked quietly. The army still had their guns trained on them.

"I can't do it," Roman said. Aries wasn't sure if he meant that he couldn't kill him or couldn't fight against the serum.

"It's okay. Listen to me. Just drop the knife."

"I can't." Roman was breathing heavily. Aries felt Roman's hands tremble.

"Yes, you can. Like this." Aries dropped his gun and kicked it away.

"Sir, you just kicked your only defense away," a soldier said.

"No, I didn't. Because Roman won't kill me. Right, Roman? You're gonna put the knife down," Aries said quietly and calmly.

"If I put the knife down, I'll choke you," Roman said. Aries thought about his options. Truthfully, he could get out of a chokehold, but if Roman had a knife in his hand the chances of accidentally getting stabbed were higher. If Roman dropped the knife, he had a safer escape plan.

"Okay! Yeah, you can do that. Alright. Here's what's gonna happen. My friend, Roman, is going to put his knife down and when he does that, get him off of me and get him to the medic on my ship. Okay? Roman is just a little sick right now. He doesn't actually want to hurt me," Aries announced.

"Aries, I don't like this," Marko said.

"Roman does not actually want to hurt me," Aries firmly repeated.

Roman's hand trembled as he struggled to toss the knife away. As soon as his hand was free, he wrapped it around Aries's throat. Aries struggled to get Roman off of him. Roman got Aries to his knees and was still strangling him. His brother was the first to run up to pull him away, shouting at him to let go. Roman finally let go and landed a punch on Aries's face.

"Get him to Besnik. Don't hurt him. He's not in his right mind," Aries said, gasping and rubbing his jaw. Elenora ran up and hugged her dad.

"That was scary. I didn't like that," she said.

"Yeah, well, it was their last-ditch effort to try to take me out. It's over though. It's all over," Aries said, hugging his daughter back. The people of Eris slowly emerged from their safe spots and looked around. Robots and people laid dead from the battle. But ultimately, it was over. There were no more of the queen's robots on their planet. There wasn't any reason to fear the queen or follow her rule. They were freed.

"Who's the leader here?" Aries asked. Everyone looked around waiting for someone to say something.

The Broken Kingdom of Orion

"We don't have one anymore," someone shouted. "You are!"

"No, I'm not staying. I was here to get rid of the bots, and now I have to go," Aries said. The crowd shifted and Kettle and Kayo were pushed to the front.

"That farm boy. He started this whole revolution thing. He's gonna lead us," someone said, pushing Kettle towards Aries. Kettle looked at Aries with fear.

"Hi Kettle!" Elenora said.

"Elenora? You…I...What?" Kettle stammered.

"This is my dad, Aries. And we just freed this planet from my mom, the evil Queen Nava," Elenora informed him. A few people looked around, nervously waiting for a robot to appear and cause problems, but none did.

"We truly are freed," someone said. People began to cheer. The people began to chant Aries's name over and over to praise their hero. Aries wasn't quite sure how to handle this. On one hand, he really wanted the moral redemption that came with saving a planet. People had cheered his name every time he entered a room on Orion. On the other hand, he was no hero. He did what anyone in his position would do. He never even thought about his own reward. He wanted to do what was right.

"Kettle, is it? Kettle, do you want to rule Eris?" Aries asked.

"Oh, umm, not really."

"Yes, he does. He just doesn't know it," Kayo said. She slipped her hand into Kettle's and clung to him.

"Kayo," Elenora scoffed. Kayo glanced at Elenora and smirked.

"My new boyfriend rules a whole planet," she bragged.

"That's cute. My dad is the king of his whole planet and just freed your planet from enslavement," Elenora retorted. Kettle sighed.

"Play nice, ladies."

"Kettle, Kayo, if you want you can return to Earth. We're taking the kids back since the whole thing was a manipulation scam," The General said.

"Thanks for the offer but we need to stay here and rebuild our planet," Kayo said.

"Alright, well, if that's everything we can do here then my team is going to head out," Aries said. His crew loaded onto the ship.

"Take care of our girl, Captain Aries," The General said. Aries gave a small smile and saluted him, The General saluted back. Elenora hugged The General tightly before following her father back to the Battleship.

24: Battleship Juniper

Roman was led to the infirmary by two crewmen.

"This man needs to be restrained," one announced. Besnik looked up and rushed over to Roman.

"What happened?" he demanded.

"I-I killed Aries," Roman said. Besnik looked horrified, but the two men shook their heads.

"Aries is insistent that he was poisoned and wants him to be assessed. I want him to be restrained for safety reasons," the other crewman said. Besnik helped Roman into a bed and applied safe restraints to him.

"Hey, I like being tied down by you," Roman teased.

"Stop," Besnik demanded. The crewmen walked off when Roman was safely apprehended by Besnik. Roman grabbed Besnik's hand.

"Life's too short. I just fought in a war and killed our commander. I don't want to wait anymore. I don't want to figure myself out. I want to be with you and be who I am with you," Roman rambled. Besnik ignored him and took his blood. "Say something."

Reji Ex

"I don't have anything to say. I have to run your labs." Besnik collected his blood tubes and started to walk away.

"Wait, Besnik, please. I love you," Roman pleaded.

"Let's just see how you feel after I run your blood work," Besnik muttered. He went to the lab and ran Roman's blood. A few minutes later the computer spat out the results. Besnik read it and his heart sank.

"So, do you still love me?" Roman asked as Besnik approached his bedside.

"Roman, did the queen inject you with anything?" Besnik asked.

"Umm...not that I remember. Why?" Before Besnik could answer, Marko, Elenora, and Aries entered the room.

"How's he doing?" Marko asked.

"Aries? You're alive? But I stabbed you," Roman said. Aries took out his dart gun and shot Roman in the forehead. "Ow. Thank you, Captain."

"Roman was injected with something. It's custom-made for him, specifically. It merged itself into his DNA. I'll have to custom make an antidote," Besnik explained. Aries looked at Roman. He lunged at Aries, but the restraints held him down. Aries shot him with another dart.

"Aries, stop," Marko said under his breath.

"He's trying to kill me first," Aries whispered back.

"I feel fine. I feel like myself, but then I just get the overwhelming urge to..." Roman started.

"It's mind control or brainwashing. Whatever you want to call it. No one's holding this against you," Aries told Roman. Roman shifted against his restraints and laughed nervously.

"That's a relief."

Reji Ex

Aries shifted his attention away from Roman. "I've seen this before, Besnik. None of them ever recovered from whatever it was."

"Well, if it alters DNA, it wouldn't be fixable," Elenora said.

"I'll have to experiment with his blood and different medications. It could take weeks. But the worst case is he'll have to take daily medication to combat the urge to kill Aries," Besnik said.

"I don't understand. He was completely fine until—" Aries cut Marko off.

"Until that bot said his trigger code. I'm sorry, Roman. She clearly did this on Ceres. I should have gotten you out sooner."

Roman laughed hysterically. "My suicide mission turned me into a sleeper agent. How cliché."

"Alright, rest up, Roman. I'm gonna need you for the next battle," Aries said. He left the room with Elenora and Marko.

"What if I don't ever get better? I'll have to be in restraints forever. What am I gonna do?" Roman ranted. Besnik ran his fingers through Roman's hair and gently kissed his lips, then planted another gentle kiss on his forehead.

"Relax, and let me take care of you," Besnik said. Roman leaned against him.

Besnik held him as long as he could before he needed to begin his lab work to find a cure for Roman.

Aries led the group to the kitchen.

"What are we doing here?" Marko asked.

"Food," Aries simply stated. He got pans and ingredients out to start cooking.

"What does a king know about cooking?" Marko asked. Aries stopped for a moment but then continued.

Reji Ex

"Marko, food is an easy way to make the brain feel like it's safe. Aries is feeding us because he wants us to feel safe after the war we just won," Vine said.

"That's right," Aries said.

"Like how girls eat a ton of ice cream because men are traumatizing," Vine added.

"Exactly," Elenora said.

"I traumatize you?" Marko asked.

"Anyways, I figured since you are my new trusted advisors while my other ones are preoccupied, I would let you know the current plan," Aries started.

"Were you taking me back to Earth?" Vine asked.

"Of course, I said I was going to, and nothing has changed that. I just figured that, if you were willing, I could use your skills to help liberate a few more planets," Aries said. Vine smiled at Aries.

"Sure. I would love to be the person responsible for liberating planets. And you and I can get to know each other more on the way," Vine said.

"Vine! Stop trying to sleep with my dad!" Elenora said.

"I'm not! You should always know the team you're working with," Vine protested.

"Oh, well, if that's the case you and I can go talk to my brother after dinner," Marko suggested. Vine glared at Marko, who just laughed.

Aries watched his daughter and her friends with amusement. They were teasing each other and laughing and joking. The trauma of war was completely ineffective to them. He secretly envied how easy it was for them to remain cheerful and happy. They had each other to help. Aries had been on his own for so long. He didn't have to hurt

The Broken Kingdom of Orion

anymore. He didn't have to be alone. Times were changing and Aries wasn't sure if it was for better or for worse. When Aries was done cooking, he served his kids and turned to leave.

"Aren't you eating too?" Elenora asked. He looked over his shoulder at her.

"I have some business to take care of, but I'll be right back," Aries said. He walked out, and the kids ate their dinner.

Aries made his way down to his prison cells. He observed that his cells were cleaner and all-around nicer than Nava's. His cells were empty, as he rarely took and kept prisoners unless they were truly evil. He wished he had a cigar with him, but he remembered he told Elenora that he would cut back. He stopped in front of Jax's cell.

"You know, you're not who I thought you were," Jax said.

"Oh, no? And why is that?" Aries asked. Jax shrugged.

"I was told the same thing everyone else was. Aries is a bloodthirsty pirate that kills without a second thought. And look at you. You had that whole speech planned out in your head to execute me and at the end, you showed me mercy," Jax said.

"So what? You want me to kill you?"

"No, the truth is, I don't think you're capable of killing."

"I've killed people who've said that to me."

"No, I think I know the real Aries. Or Dante, I should say. You're just a broken man. I don't think you've truly killed anyone. I don't think you have it in you."

"Oh, you're wrong. The thing about being a powerful empath, you can feel the fear that radiates off of your victims. There's anger with it. Always anger.

Reji Ex

But overwhelming fear and dread. And you know what? It physically hurts, those strong emotions they feel. But one cap and that pain is all gone. And that's so liberating," Aries said.

"So, you are just a murderer. Then why not me?" Jax asked.

"I know that you know where she is," Aries said simply.

Jax scoffed and nodded. "You think that I'll betray the queen?"

"I do. There was a reason you were on Eris and willing to die. She was no longer protecting you," Aries said.

"She's on Makemake," Jax answered quickly, looking away.

"That's all I needed to know." Aries turned on his heels to leave. Jax jumped up and went to the bars of his cell.

"You're still chasing her. You're still hunting her. Your goal is to end her, then what? Will it be enough for you to heal your broken soul?" Jax taunted.

"Yes. I believe it will." Aries started to walk away.

"I think you blame yourself for Orion. You brought her there and she blew it up. You couldn't protect them," Jax called after Aries. Aries closed the door behind him as he left. Jax was right about that. Aries had always blamed himself for Orion. Aries went back to the kitchen and sat down with the kids.

"So, I was thinking. Makemake needs to be liberated. If you're willing to join me, that is," Aries said. Elenora smiled at her father.

"I'm always with you," she said.

"I go with Elenora, so I guess I'm in," Marko said. "Plus, you'll need extra med staff if Besnik is gonna be taking care of Roman."

"Well, it would be nice to visit home again before going to Earth forever," Vine said.

"Alright, sounds like we all agree then," Aries said with a smile. They continued with dinner, joking and laughing and acting like a

The Broken Kingdom of Orion

normal family. For once, Aries felt calm. He was feeling their happiness. He just hoped that they were this happy after they took out Nava on Makemake. Aries was never going to tell them the real reason why they were going to Makemake. His motivation was corrupt.

He would not rest until the queen is brought to justice for her crimes.

He would not rest until the people of Orion were avenged.

He would not rest until Nava was dead.

Acknowledgments

I would like to give a special thank you to my editor, Sage. I don't even need to mention how important the publishers have been on this journey but I will anyways just in case: A very special thank you to Misti and everyone else in Flick-It-Books who made this possible. And all though he can't be here for this, a special thank you to Sam.

About the Author

Reji Ex is from a small town in Pennsylvania. She is the mother of one and a semi-loving wife to her lifelong partner in crime, Jacob. She is also a mom to two orphaned kittens and a terrible dog. She attempted a degree in Secondary English Education but finally graduated college with an associate's degree in Veterinary Medicine, which isn't even being used.

Reji has been writing since she was in middle school as a method to cope with anxiety and depression. Her love for space started around the same time when her science mentor bought her a model rocket. She has taught 4H kids the basics of model rocketry. Her other hobbies include acting, singing, and art.

Printed by BoD™in Norderstedt, Germany